THE TEST OF TRUTH

DEFIANCE #4

JASON KRUMBINE

Published by Lantern Key Books

ISBN: 978-1-971197-03-6

Originally published in 2019 by Jason Krumbine

First Lantern Key Books Edition: December 2025

about this book

A hundred years ago the Veneer Empire was one of the strongest members of the UPA.

And then the Unity attacked.

In the devastating aftermath, the Veneer Empire withdrew from the UPA and hasn't been heard from since.

Ambassador Caldwell Reynoso is the latest in a long line of dignitaries who spend their days waiting until the Veneer are ready to communicate again. While it is not a lifetime appointment, Ambassador Reynoso will not hold any other position before his untimely death.

*When an ambassador dies, the political ramifications can be complicated. When an ambassador is **murdered**, the ramifications can be disastrous.*

As the mystery of who murdered Ambassador Reynoso slowly unravels, Captain Mitchell and the crew of the Defiance find themselves sitting on a powder keg of galactic proportions. And unless they can stop it, when it goes off, it's going to take half the galaxy with it.

Books in the Defiance Series

Defiance
Hand of God
Act of God
The Test of Truth
The Price of Paradise
The Value of Terror
The Last Breath of a Dying Tomorrow

Subscribe to my newsletter and I'll let you know as soon as the next Defiance book is ready to read.

https://onestrayword.beehiiv.com/subscribe

THE TEST OF TRUTH

Dispatched to investigate a mysterious SOS signal transmitted in a code that hadn't been used in hundreds of years the Defiance stumbles across a vessel from another universe entirely and find themselves woefully unprepared for a savage Unity attack.

After Captain Mitchell dispatches a boarding party to investigate, he's visited by an all-powerful entity named Steve.

According to an all-powerful entity named Steve, the Defiance's universe is simply one of many, stacked atop one other. Steve is from the top of the Stack. The Unity is from the bottom and it's slowly working its way up, consuming every universe in its path. He warns Mitchell that the Unity is an inevitability.

To convince Mitchell of his power, Steve sends Lieutenant Zemble to another dimension where time passes differently. It is not currently known what Zemble experienced in this other dimension, beyond the fact that it was traumatic.

During the Unity attack Commander Cayden Keane is nearly killed, losing two of his limbs and is beyond the help of the Defiance's medical capabilities. Sharon, the sister/lover to Steve, appears and restores Keane completely. In addition to healing him from the Unity attack, she also heals his injuries from the decades-old incident at Serenity Base. According to Doctor Dheer and the ship's computer, every missing body part on Keane has been restored and he has the body, health and stamina of fit and healthy twenty-five-year-old, despite being nearly a decade older.

Lieutenant Commander Nax has been hallucinating his dead

girlfriend, Grace Hawkins. No one on the Defiance is aware of this save for Chief Engineer Warrick, who simply suspects there might be something wrong with his friend.

In the aftermath of the Unity attack and confrontation with Steve and Sharon, the Defiance has returned to Starbase Atlantic for much needed repairs.

1

USS DEFIANCE

DOCKED AT STARBASE ATLANTIC

"You know what I liked?"

Nax didn't answer with words. He simply made a vague, questioning noise from the back of his throat.

"That time we took shore leave on Baftal Prime."

Nax turned his head to look at Hawkins. She laid on the bed next to him, naked. Her hand resting on his bare chest, a sharp contrast of brilliant white against his orange skin. Her leg entwined itself with his and she snuggled in closer.

"As I recall, we both contracted Zixens," Nax said, brushing his fingers through her dark brown hair. "We didn't leave our hotel room the entire time."

"I know." Hawkins smiled. "It was nice."

Nax frowned. "We were regurgitating every meal."

"That part, obviously, wasn't the nice part."

"Which part was?" Nax asked. "Would it be when we suffered momentary blindness for twenty minutes every afternoon?"

"No." She idly stroked her fingers across his chest.

Nax nodded his head. "Then perhaps it was the glowing diarrhea?"

She lightly smacked at him. "Okay, stop it."

"I am simply trying to determine what part of that experience you found to be nice," Nax said. "Most people who contract Zixens describe it as the most painful and intolerable experience of their lives. I have read more than one report of victims who have suffered at the hands of the Oxean Syndicate and they've claimed they would rather be enslaved by the Oxeans again before contracting Zixens a second time."

Hawkins propped her head up on the palm of her other hand in order to look him in the eye. "You're doing this on purpose, aren't you?"

"I don't know what you're talking about," Nax replied. His expression deadpan.

"You should know that I know you better than you know yourself at this point," Hawkins said.

"I would certainly hope so."

"I know when you're pulling my leg, is what I'm trying to say."

His gaze flicked down to her bare leg that was entwined with his. Hawkins took her hand from his chest and gently lifted his chin so that their eyes met again.

"Stop it." Her voice was playful.

"Your opening thesis was that our time on Baftal Prime was one of your favorites," he said.

"No. I said that I *liked* our time on Baftal Prime," Hawkins corrected him.

"I fail to see the difference," Nax said. "Considering that in either version, we were both still sick with Zixens."

Hawkins sighed. "You know what I like about you?"

"I'm still not certain what you liked about the time I was so overcome with nausea I was unable to leave the bathroom for nearly three hours."

She poked at his nose. "Your commitment to a bit. Other people don't like it. Warrick, for example, finds it extremely irritating."

"Warrick is my closest and oldest friend."

"Which would explain why he's so bothered by it," she said. "I, however, find it charming."

"But, perhaps, by your logic, that's because you simply haven't known me long enough."

"I suppose that's true," Hawkins conceded. "Or maybe I just know you better than Warrick does? I mean, I've certainly seen more of you than he has."

"That's not entirely true."

"I beg your pardon?"

"Warrick and I spent a season in a colony on New Gazaya that was...averse to the notion of clothing."

"I'm sorry, what?"

A puzzled expression passed across Nax's face. "You don't know?"

"Should I?" she deflected.

He didn't answer for a moment, searching her eyes for something he wasn't certain of.

"I'm not a mind reader," Hawkins said with a playful smile.

"No, of course not."

"I only know what you want me to know."

"Obviously."

"You don't sound convinced."

"You're reminiscing about a joint event in our lives where we were both so sick that simply touching each other trigged violent, nauseous reactions."

She laughed softly and dropped her head onto his chest.

"That reaction isn't helping my confusion."

"How long were you and Warrick hanging out in this nudist colony?"

Nax didn't answer right away. His fingers caressed her dark hair and he stared off into the distance. "Only a few months,"

"So, what? The two of you just hung around naked?"

"More or less."

"What were you doing on New Gazaya in the first place?"

"Struggling with the consequences of poor decisions," he replied flatly.

She laughed again.

"What?" Nax asked.

"I just love you," Hawkins replied. "That's all."

Nax didn't say anything.

She turned her head so that she could look into his eyes. "Did I catch you off guard with that?"

"No," Nax said. "Not exactly."

"Just what every girl wants to hear."

"This isn't something we've discussed before," Nax said.

"It was bound to come up eventually."

"Now?"

"It's okay," she said, tracing her finger along his collarbone. "You don't have to say it. I know how you feel about me."

"I thought you weren't a mind reader."

"I'm not. But I don't have to read your mind to know that. That's what I liked about that time on Baftal Prime."

"I was wondering when we were going to get back to that."

"That's when I knew you loved me."

Nax didn't look convinced.

Hawkins caressed a finger along the side of his cheek. "Come on, this can't be that much of a surprise to you."

"There seems to be no end to things about you that surprise me," Nax said.

She smiled. "That's cute. And, see, if that had come from anybody else, I might be worried."

"But you're not."

"Of course not."

"Because?"

"Because how else do you explain the fact that you had any interest in me after four days of seeing shit coming out of my mouth and ass at the same time?"

Nax winced uncomfortably.

Hawkins smiled impishly. "It's not like there's a more delicate way to describe it."

"There should be."

"It's okay."

"It's really not," he said.

"I'm happy with how it turned out," Hawkins said. "I think that's the real moral of the story."

Nax moved his hand to cup her cheek. She closed her eyes and nuzzled into his palm. He didn't say anything for a minute and then, almost in a whisper, he said, "Me too."

She opened her eyes. "Are you sure?"

For a brief moment there was a genuine look of...fear? Concern? Nax couldn't tell.

The communicator on the nightstand chirped.

"Go on," she said.

"I can ignore it," he said.

"Sure," she agreed. "But that just means somebody will either end up knocking on your door. Or, worse, calling you over the ship's intercom."

"I have a fairly high threshold for embarrassment."

"Sure. That's why you have a bad habit of answering the door naked," Hawkins said with a smirk. "I, however, don't share that threshold."

The communicator on the nightstand chirped again and Nax reluctantly rolled away from Hawkins, answering it with a soft sigh. "Yes?"

"You in the middle of anything important?" Warrick asked his voice booming over the communicator.

Nax turned back to Hawkins, but she was gone. Her side of the bed was empty once again. The sheets were undisturbed as if she had never been there, because, of course, she hadn't.

Nax sighed again and closed his eyes. "No," he replied.

"Then get your ass down here," Warrick said. "Westin's driving me crazy and the rest of my staff are about as useful as a collection of Vulderran ass farts. I need a hand from somebody who's not a high functioning idiot."

2

"NOW THE SERPENT was more cunning than any beast of the field which the Lord God had made," Zemble spoke softly as he read aloud to the comatose woman on the bed in front of him. "And he said to the woman, 'Has God indeed said, 'You shall not eat of every tree of the garden'?' And the woman said to the serpent, 'We may eat the fruit of the trees of the garden; but of the fruit of the tree which is in the midst of the garden, God has said, 'You shall not eat it, nor shall you touch it, lest you die." Then the serpent said to the woman, 'You will not surely die. For God knows that in the day you eat of it your eyes will be opened, and you will be like God, knowing good and evil.'"

A noise at the door caused Zemble to stop and look up. Lt. Commander Sadie Sadler stood in the doorway, looking slightly embarrassed. "Sorry," she said quietly. "I didn't mean to interrupt." She pointed back over her shoulder. "I was looking for Marlize and I heard something in here. I thought..." She trailed off, glancing at the comatose woman and then awkwardly back at Zemble.

In the small room, the Elwat looked almost twice as

large. Zemble thumbed off his datapad and set it on the small table next to the bed. "You thought Erin Calloway had regained consciousness and suddenly sounded like an adult male Elwat?"

Sadler laughed softly and rubbed her eyes. "Okay, well, in my defense I'm still not getting any sleep."

"Bad dreams?"

Sadler sighed, blowing out her cheeks. "I wish. Long shifts and too much work. I'll be glad when the new XO comes on board."

"I have a feeling that's just going to create more problems," Zemble said.

"Maybe," Sadler agreed. "But they won't be my problems."

"I have it on good authority that the new first officer is being appointed by the D'Ambra administration," Zemble said. "Which means I can almost guarantee you that he isn't going to have Directive Fifty-Two clearance."

"Still doesn't sound like it's going to be my problem."

"As the next ranking officer with Directive Fifty-Two clearance you're essentially a shadow first officer to Captain Mitchell."

"*Shadow* first officer?" Sadler repeated in disbelief.

"I'm making an educated guess here."

"Shadow first officer?" Sadler repeated again.

"It sounds worse than it is."

"Are you sure about that? Because it sounds pretty bad. It sounds like you're suggesting that the captain is running a secret secondary command crew here."

Zemble shrugged. "An educated guess."

"Seriously?"

"I guess if you want something more concrete you might want to check in with Keane," Zemble suggested. "If there was a shadow command crew, he would definitely be in on it."

Sadler shook her head. "I can't believe this."

"Sure you can," Zemble said.

"I didn't ask for this."

"I don't think that matters," Zemble said.

"It should," Sadler said. "My career path wasn't supposed to include getting drafted into some top-secret spy agency inside the UPA."

"That's only because you didn't know about it until you got recruited," Zemble said.

"I would love to go back to not knowing about it."

"Is that why you're looking for Doctor Dheer? Because I don't think she specializes in memory altering."

"No, but she's a pretty decent drinking partner."

"Not a bad place to start," Zemble said. "But if you're looking to kill off a few brain cells, may I suggest Chief Engineer Warrick? He has a much better palate for exotic alcohol."

"I don't think there's enough alcohol in the world to make me forget about Steve and Sharon."

Zemble grunted. "Agreed."

Sadler sighed.

"To answer your question, I haven't seen Doctor Dheer," Zemble said.

"Right. Right. Okay. Well..." Sadler nodded at the data-pad. "Genesis?"

"You're familiar with the Bible?"

Sadler shrugged. "Unfortunately."

He looked at her questioningly.

"It's a long story about my childhood and over-involved parents that I'd really rather not get into," Sadler said.

"Fair enough," Zemble said.

"Somebody told me you've been coming down here every day."

Zemble just grunted in response, pressing his hands together. He rested his chin on the back of his knuckles as he watched Calloway's chest steadily rise and fall with each breath.

"Why Genesis?"

"I wanted to skip ahead to the New Testament," he admitted. "But I was afraid she'd be lost without the back-story." He nodded at Calloway. "Besides, you can never go wrong starting at the beginning."

"So you're just going to sit here and read her the entire Bible?"

"It can't hurt her."

"There's no guarantee it's going to help either."

Zemble turned to her, not saying anything.

"Lapsed Christian," Sadler said. "Sorry. My faith's in short supply these days."

Zemble turned back to Calloway. "There are worse things to be."

Sadler raised both eyebrows, but didn't know what to say to that.

"Sometimes I just come down here and pray with her," Zemble said.

"You think she can hear you?"

"Rabkin says she can't."

"That's not what I asked."

"She's not the one I'm worried about hearing my prayers."

Sadler nodded. "You're a good person."

"No, I'm not."

"Nobody else is coming down here."

"I think that speaks more to everybody else's behavior than it does to mine."

Sadler sighed and rubbed the side of her face. "Okay. Look, I'm just saying, it's a nice thing."

Zemble looked at her out of the corner of his eye. "Considering she's not going to wake up."

Sadler frowned. "I didn't say that."

"You didn't have to. It's what everybody's saying."

"If you're looking to pick a fight, I'm going to leave because I've got enough on my plate and now I'm going to be worried about strange men approaching me with code phrases and secret missions. Last thing I need is to get drawn into some kind of a morality debate with *you*."

Zemble grumbled something unintelligible and sat back. The chair groaned imperceptibly under the movement. "Sorry."

"Don't worry about it," she said with a wave of her hand. "I get it."

"I doubt that." Zemble got to his feet, picking up the datapad.

"You're worried that it feels like God isn't answering your prayers," she said, following him out into the main medbay.

Zemble glanced over his shoulder at her.

"There's a reason my faith is in short supply," Sadler said as they stepped out into the corridor.

Zemble frowned and turned to her, folding his arms. "That's not what I'm worried about."

"Oh?"

"God's under no obligation to answer my prayers," Zemble said. "He's God and I'm not."

"That's certainly one way of looking at it," Sadler muttered.

"And even still, a 'No' is still an answer," Zemble continued.

"Okay, sure," Sadler said. "I suppose that's true."

"But that's not my problem," Zemble said.

"Okay?"

"My problem's a little more complicated," Zemble said. "Why did this have to happen to Erin?"

"Bad things happen to good people all the time," Sadler said. "It's just the way of the universe. This can't possibly be news to you."

Zemble nodded and held out his hands, palms open. "Sure. But *why*?"

Sadler gesticulated with her hands for a moment. "I don't know how I'm supposed to answer that. I don't think anybody knows how to answer that. It's just one of those questions that can't be answered."

"I don't believe that."

"I'm sorry?"

"There's an answer for everything."

"Is there?"

"Absolutely. Everything happens for a reason and a lot of those reasons are because God said so."

Sadler scratched the back of her head. "Well, okay. Then we're getting into an area where you're questioning God's reasoning."

Zemble nodded, clasping his hands behind his back. "It would certainly seem so."

3

"I FEEL as though I shouldn't have to mention this, but it's not safe to be holding that wire in your mouth like that." Nax looked pointedly at the thick, frayed, yellow wire that Warrick was holding down between his teeth.

Warrick looked at him with a dull expression of irritation and held up his two hands that were already full as if to say 'I haven't grown a third hand yet, so what do you want me to do?'

Nax held out his hand and Warrick opened his mouth, letting the wire drop into the orange man's grip. If Nax was bothered or disgusted by the saliva dripping from the wire, he gave no sign.

He did, however, twitch a little bit as the wire made contact with his open palm and a slight electrical current jolted his body.

"Careful," Warrick said. "It's a hot wire."

Nax's left hand twitched again and he carefully moved his fingers away from its frayed, exposed sections.

Nax had found Warrick in the lower deck of engineering wearing a uniform that looked like it was covered in electrical burns and smelled even worse. He was surrounded by a mess of equipment, cables and broken floor plates.

With a hot wire handed off to Nax, Warrick busied himself with the alcubierre field coils that were already occupying his hands. He turned in a half circle, searching the mess of equipment for something.

"Should I be concerned?" Nax asked.

"Should *you* be concerned?"

"I've counted no less than six different ways you could kill yourself right now," Nax said. "Not intentionally, of course. Just through pure, irresponsible neglect."

Warrick stopped looking and turned back to Nax. "Excuse me?"

"Well, for starters," Nax said and carefully held up the wire that had previously been held in Warrick's mouth.

"Do I look like a damn Sweezakaal stripper?" Warrick asked.

"Obviously not," Nax replied evenly.

"Then what the hell are you talking about?" Warrick tossed Nax one of the coils.

Nax easily caught the coil. "You literally just exemplified what I was talking about."

Warrick waved him off, kneeling down next to a pile of broken plasma conduits. "I've been working around the clock for the last two weeks trying to get this ship back to something that's at least vaguely reminiscent of something that's space worthy. And you know what I have to show for it? Half of deck three still has no power. Somehow our targeting systems got completely deleted and now have to be rebuilt from the ground up. Our hull breach on deck ten still isn't patched up and the gravity plating on the starboard side is so out of whack that if you take one step, you'll end up flying across the corridor." He exhaled. "I swear, this ship is going to be the death of us all." He shoved a collection of dirty rags out of the way, exposing an open floor panel. "What did you say to Rabkin?"

"Nothing," Nax replied, carefully setting the alcubierre field coil down on the floor next to him. "As I only just became aware of your suicidal tendencies. You can rest assured that I'll be speaking with him as soon as I've determined you're not going to get yourself killed once I leave."

There was a loud electrical surge as Warrick yanked a thick cable from underneath a floor panel. The lights above them flickered and somebody on the upper levels yelped.

"Ha," Warrick muttered under his breath, grinning as he plugged the cable into the alcubierre field coil he still held. "I swear, nobody in this damn department knows the first thing about basic engineering. This ship would be a thousand times better if it was just me running things down here."

"I question that logic," Nax said.

"I don't," Warrick said. "Westin nearly blew out half the convertors on deck six because she crossed plasma fuses." He pulled out a scanner from his hip pocket and doubled checked the readings. "No, I meant what did you say to Rabkin about *your* condition?" There was a soft ping from the scanner and Warrick shoved the cable and coil back under the floor panel before securing it back in place. Once that was done, he turned to Nax expectantly. "Well?"

To anyone else, Nax would have appeared unperturbed, but not to Warrick.

Nax met Warrick's gaze evenly and without hesitation.

Neither of them spoke for several moments. Above them there was a shower of sparks followed by another yelp.

Warrick pointed his scanner at Nax. "You're thinking about lying to me."

"I am not," Nax insisted.

"You're thinking that maybe you can convince me what happened on the *Eternal Hand of God* didn't really happen."

"The thought never crossed my mind."

"Bullshit it didn't," Warrick said.

"I am beginning to think you didn't call me down here for my assistance," Nax said. "Is the rest of your engineering crew even partially incompetent?"

"Of course not," Warrick said. "But Westin's like a damn virus. Half the people she talks to end up dumber than a Uboklu princess."

"That sounds like a serious problem."

"Not as serious as Fey's Euphoria," Warrick said.

Nax visibly winced.

"Your poker face don't look so good."

"I would rather you not use that phrase so openly."

"And I would rather my friend not try to bullshit me."

Nax frowned. "It's not Fey's."

Warrick's eyes widened in surprise. "Oh? And who gave you that diagnosis? Because last time I checked, we haven't been back to Natuzzi and there's not one damn doctor in the entire Fleet that even *knows* about Fey's Euphoria."

"Then obviously it would be pointless for me to speak with Rabkin about it," Nax said.

"That wasn't the agreement."

"I don't believe we made an agreement."

"Do not pull this crap with me."

"I don't know what you want me to say, Jaxson."

"I want you to tell me that you spoke with Rabkin."

"Then I would be lying," Nax said. "And you clearly just told me not to lie to you."

Warrick held up his scanner. "I swear, if beating you over

the head with this would actually fix anything, I would do it in a heartbeat."

"And I would let you do it in a heartbeat," Nax said. "The fact of the matter is that the situation resolved itself before I needed to speak with Rabkin about it."

"It *resolved* itself?"

"I do not believe I stuttered."

"You're lying to me," Warrick said.

"No, I am not."

"The hell you aren't. Fey's-"

"It is *not* Fey's," Nax snapped, cutting him off.

"Then what is it?" Warrick asked.

Nax inhaled through his nose. "It was simply some mild sleep deprivation that resulted in momentary hallucinations."

"Sounds a lot like Fey's Euphoria."

"Except that I can still tell the difference between what is real and what isn't," Nax said.

"I wouldn't be so quick to promise that," Hawkins said from behind him. Nax resisted the urge to look at her. "I'm not going to lie. Watching you dance around like this? This is amazing. Technically nothing you've said is untrue. I mean, you know, except for the part where you're not losing your mind. But everything else? It's all technically true. That's kind of impressive. I didn't realize you had it in you."

Warrick sighed and took a step back, leaning against the wall for support. He ran a hand over his bald head. "Nax..."

"Fey's is not something to be discussed outside of Natuzzi," Nax said. "This is a sensitive subject. You swore an oath."

"You reminded me of that already."

"And apparently I need to remind you again."

"I'm trying to look out for you," Warrick said. "Why are you fighting me on this?"

"I cannot be diagnosed with Fey's," Nax said. "Never mind the political implications of an off-planet Natuzzi being discovered with a crippling disease that affects nearly forty percent of the Natuzzi population. The simple fact of the matter is that I cannot be diagnosed with something I do not have."

"Is that what the doctors back on Natuzzi would say if they examined you?" Warrick asked.

"We're not on Natuzzi right now."

"I know damn well where we are."

"So there's no point in discussing what might happen in a location where we currently are not," Nax said.

Warrick shook his head. "Why are you doing this?"

"Because it's the truth."

"I'm going to ask you one question, Nax, and I would rather you not lie to me," Warrick said. "If nothing else, tell me the truth on this: Are you still seeing Grace?"

Hawkins stepped up next to Nax and folded her arms. "Well, that just gets right to the heart of the matter, doesn't it?"

Nax ignored her, keeping his gaze focused on Warrick. "No," he replied without hesitation.

"Ouch," Hawkins said with a wince. "That actually stings a little." She held up a hand and closely examined it. "I wonder, if you deny me enough, will I just fade away completely? Do you think you'll have to clap your hands and say, 'I believe!' in order to bring me back?"

Nax took a step forward, putting Hawkins behind him again. "I haven't seen Grace since the *Eternal Hand of God*. And as you've no doubt already heard; I haven't been engaged in any ancient Natuzzi grieving rituals."

"Much to my disappointment," Hawkins said. "I kind of enjoyed those. You have a beautiful voice, you know."

Nax struggled to keep his expression neutral. "I've been sleeping again. Perhaps not as well as before, but it's still a restful period for me. Everything is fine. Everything is normal. I am not sick. I promise you."

"Well, that is definitely a promise you are not going to keep," Hawkins whispered into his ear.

Warrick's face was impassive. He didn't say anything.

And before he could say anything, Commander Cayden Keane popped through the nearest doorway with a wide grin on his face. "Just the two men I was looking for."

Keane was either oblivious to the tension in the room or chose to ignore it. Neither Nax nor Warrick could tell.

"What's wrong now?" Warrick asked. "Do the ion cannons need to be recalibrated again?"

"Don't know. Don't care." Keane clapped his hands together. "I don't know if either of you gentlemen know this, but I've got myself a brand-new liver. It's like it's right off the assembly line. It's still got that new liver smell to it and I am itching to break it in. I'm looking for a few good men to help me out. I've got excellent intel that suggests that at least one pub on the *Atlantic* is serving some new Backlon whiskey, which is all but guaranteed to put hair on your chest." He held out his hands. "I also have it on good authority that the both of you are supposed to be off duty right now."

"I haven't been off duty since we docked," Warrick said.

"Which is why you're supposed to be off duty now," Keane said. "I mean, seriously, you look like shit."

"I'm trying to keep this bucket of bolts from falling apart and leaving us all to the cold, unforgiving merciless void of space," Warrick said.

"Yeah, you definitely need to take a break," Keane said.

"Where's Zemble?" Warrick asked.

"Don't know. Don't care," Keane replied. "Besides, he's a teetotaler and buzzkill."

Warrick glanced at Nax wordlessly who refused to meet his gaze. Warrick grunted and tossed the scanner into the pile of equipment. "Sure. What the hell. Ship's not going to fall apart tonight. Let's get wasted."

Keane turned, headed for the corridor. "Amen to that, brother."

4

STARBASE ATLANTIC

ZEMBLE STOOD in the wide empty corridor of E Deck feeling strangely lost as he stared at the empty outline of where the cross used to sit above the doors. Zemble looked around, hoping to find somebody to ask what he already knew, but of course, there was no one else nearby. At this hour the population of the *Atlantic* was either focused on their respective duties or asleep. His back was to the railing that overlooked the main public promenade of the *Atlantic*, with six rings stretching up from G deck all the way to D Deck, containing a variety of shops, restaurants, and services. So no, there was nobody around. Not that it mattered, since it was pretty clear what had happened.

His church was gone and nobody had bothered to tell him.

Zemble focused on the missing cross, wondering if there was some kind of obvious allegorical metaphor he was missing. They hadn't been gone for very long. The contrast between where the cross had been and the rest of the wall was still too sharp. So a few weeks? Surely no more than a month at most. Probably less. Beneath the missing cross, the doors were clearly shuttered and there was no note explaining why everything had been closed up.

Zemble frowned and folded his arms. This was not...ideal.

"My friend, I hope you don't mind me saying so, but you look a little lost."

Zemble turned in the direction of the voice, doing his best not to appear startled. The voice belonged to a tall, narrow man with dark hair that ended in a sharp widow's peak. He was dressed in a black suit with a single unbroken line of white that encircled his collar and then ran down the center of his jacket. He was clearly human, but his eyes seemed almost flush with the rest of his face. There was a troubling feeling at the back of Zemble's mind as he looked at the man. He couldn't put his finger on it exactly. He didn't have enough details, enough data. But, nevertheless, he knew a suspicious character when he saw one.

Zemble turned back to the shuttered doors and missing cross, not bothering with anything more than a grunt in response.

Unable to apparently take a hint, the man asked, "Anything I can help you with?"

"Not unless you know where my church went."

"Ah. Yes." The man nodded. "The Atlantic Community Church. They closed down a few months back. Are you a former parishioner?"

"Something like that," Zemble replied. He took a step closer to the shuttered doors, hoping to find a note or some indication of where they might have moved to. He hoped this would deter the man from speaking anymore and encourage him to leave. He was a suspicious character, but the only mystery Zemble was interested in solving right now was the one of what happened to his church.

"But you're not a local?" The man continued, studying Zemble's uniform. "From one of the UPA ships perhaps?" he paused, as if giving Zemble a chance to respond. When he didn't, he asked, "So you didn't hear?"

Zemble couldn't help himself. He turned back to the man. "Hear about what?"

The man stepped up so that he was standing next to Zemble. Something about his body language shifted. He didn't look at the security officer. Instead, he kept his focus on the former home of the ACC. "Well, of course, this is all secondhand knowledge to me. But, as I understand it, Pastor Loring fell on hard times."

"Hard times?" Zemble repeated.

The man nodded, clasping his hands behind his back. "Yes. Over half his congregation left." He looked at Zemble. "That certainly sounds like hard times for a man of the cloth, wouldn't you say?"

That nagging feeling at the back of Zemble's mind stirred up again. There was something in the way the man spoke...

"What happened?" Zemble asked.

The man shrugged. "Can't really say for sure. As I already explained, I heard this secondhand. But it would seem that his flock decided they didn't want to be shepherded by a man who was accused of stealing the good Lord's money."

The points of Zemble's horns tingled. It was a familiar sensation he had learned long ago to trust implicitly. He narrowed his gaze at the man. "Who did you say you were again?"

The man smiled at Zemble. "Sorry about that. It's a bad habit I just can't seem to shake. I just jump into social settings, joining whatever conversation is taking place and always forget none of these people know who I am. It's not a hubris thing, mind you. More of an absentminded professor kind of thing. I legitimately forget to introduce myself all the time. And I'm aware of it and yet I can't seem to stop myself. I'm trying to convince myself that it's just a charming character quirk. And here I am, of course, going on about it and I still haven't told you who I am." He chuckled and shook his head as if to say, 'What a dunderhead.' The man extended his hand to Zemble. "Allow me to properly introduce myself: Joseph Michael Cavige."

Zemble looked at Cavige's hand, but didn't reach for it.

The good natured smile on Cavige's face faltered a bit and he pulled back his hand. "I'm afraid I've offended you?"

"Not yet," Zemble replied.

"But you're anticipating it?"

"Force of habit."

Cavige's eyes flicked towards Zemble's dull red Fleet badge. "Ah. A man of security. Of course. You're naturally suspicious. Especially of strange men approaching you with bad news about your local church."

Zemble just grunted again.

Cavige held up both hands in what was intended to be a nonthreatening manner. "I want to assure you, Lieutenant, I am not a bad person."

"Nobody ever thinks they are," Zemble replied.

"Fair enough," Cavige agreed. "However that feels like an extreme judgment considering I'm just the bearer of bad news and not the cause of it."

"Fair enough," Zemble grunted.

Cavige took a deep breath. "I suppose I could tell you that I don't take any joy in telling you about Pastor Loring's misfortunes, but I suspect you'd have a hard time believing that, despite, of course, there being no reason to the contrary."

"Misfortunes," Zemble repeated. "Sure."

"You sound doubtful."

"Pastor Loring's a good man," Zemble said.

Cavige shrugged. "I never had the pleasure of meeting him."

Zemble turned back to the outline of the missing cross. "Then you missed out."

"It would seem so." Cavige paused. "However, even good men can have bad days."

Zemble growled faintly in the back of his throat.

Cavige quickly added, "I mean no disrespect, of course."

"That's not what it sounded like."

"Perhaps because you didn't let me finish my thought?" Cavige suggested.

"If you're trying to make me like you, you're doing a shit job."

Cavige laughed softly. "You have a way with words, Lieutenant."

"That's a polite way to say I've got a potty mouth."

Cavige shrugged. "People like to find fault with those professing to be followers of Christ."

"And is that what you're doing?" Zemble asked.

"Absolutely not," Cavige replied. He gestured to the empty promenade. "I'm simply one lost soul out for a late-night walk, trying to help another lost soul."

"I'm not lost," Zemble said.

"But you're certainly looking for something."

"Only because nobody left a forwarding address."

"It's little surprises like this that keep life interesting."

"I've got enough interesting in my life," Zemble said. "I'm not looking to add any more."

Cavige nodded. "May I make a suggestion?"

"There's no law saying that you can't," Zemble said.

Cavige chuckled. "Well, isn't that fortunate for the both of us."

Zemble watched him from the corner of his eye as he pulled a flat, rectangular card from his pocket. It was a small card, only about three inches long and two inches wide.

Cavige proffered it to Zemble. "The universe is vast and mysterious. I like to believe there's more than one way to seek guidance in it, Lieutenant."

Zemble made no effort to take the card.

Cavige nodded and placed the card in-between the slats on the shuttered doors. "I hope to see you again, Lieutenant."

Cavige quietly wandered off, not bothering to wait for a response.

Zemble leaned in closer for a better look.

The card was black with two golden interlinked triangles embossed on it. The letter C was woven between them and underneath the logo was written: Church of Eternal Clarity.

5

"*Hot damn!* That burns like a mother!" Keane smacked the empty glass back down on the table and winced painfully as the Backlon whiskey raced through his body, before settling in his gut like a tiny ball of plasma. "Shit."

Warrick grinned like a maniac as he knocked back two shots of the whiskey. He smacked his lips together appreciatively, reveling in the burning sensation. "I love it. It's like a Uboklun plasma reactor getting ready to reach critical in my gut."

The three of them sat at a small table in Dreks Tavern. Not the most respectable bar on the *Atlantic*, but then when Fleet officers were looking to get wasted, they hardly cared about being respectable when they did it.

Keane coughed, covering his mouth. "Yeah, that feels about right." He rubbed his abdomen.

"It's almost like you can feel it burning off the lining in your stomach," Warrick continued.

"Is that what that sensation is?" Keane asked.

Warrick nodded. "I once drank a dozen of these on a dare."

Keane looked at him dubiously.

"True story," Warrick assured him.

Keane glanced over at Nax at the opposite end of the table for confirmation. Nax sighed and nodded. "Unfortunately, it is a thing that happened. He also ended up in intensive care for a week afterwards."

"It was worth it to see look on that Sweezakaal bastard's face," Warrick said. "Served him right for calling me a Fim'ai ass fart."

"Yes," Nax replied coolly. "With third-degree burns over half your body and both of your legs broken, you certainly showed him."

Warrick ignored the sarcasm and said to Keane, "You didn't know what you were missing out on when you had more tellurium plastic in your body than a Fleet shuttle."

Keane nodded. "Yeah, no kidding." He glanced at Nax's untouched glass of Backlon whiskey. "You gonna drink that?"

Nax wordlessly pushed it across the table towards Keane.

"Much appreciated." Keane grabbed the shot glass and swallowed pink liquid as quickly as he could. He doubled over in his seat as his abdomen lit up in pain. He smacked his hand against the table repeatedly, riding out the pain. As it passed, he leaned back in his chair, looking up at the ceiling with watery eyes. "Oh, boy."

"Ain't that the truth," Warrick agreed.

Keane wiped his thumb and forefinger across his eyes. "I had seriously forgotten."

Warrick pointed at him. "You became a lazy drinker."

"Apparently," Keane agreed. "I thought I had this superpower."

"Having nearly half of your insides replaced with tellurium plastic is a superpower now?" Warrick asked.

"It is when you can literally drink anything you want," Keane replied. He took a deep breath, wincing as the air stung the still tender back of his throat. He looked at Warrick and Nax. "I appreciate you guys coming out with me tonight. I needed this."

Warrick clapped him on the back. "We all needed it. Westin's driving me insane. I swear, for every one thing I fix, she breaks six more. I think she's a damn jinx. I'm going to talk to the captain about getting her transferred. Maybe to the *Solomon*? I'd love to see them get laid up for something other than another refit."

Keane nodded. "I think there's a remote possibility that when the Unity attacked me, I died. Like, really died." He held up the empty glass peered closely at the few pink droplets that were still left and shrugged. "And now, sitting here like this, I kind of wonder if death has any meaning at all."

Warrick and Nax stared at him wordlessly.

Keane set the glass down and grabbed the water on the table. "It's also possible I might be more than a little drunk right now. This shit is hitting me a lot faster than I thought it was going to." He burped as if the statement needed verbal punctuation.

None of the men spoke for a minute. Keane slid his empty glasses towards the center of the table.

Warrick put a spin on his empty shot glass and sent it to join Keane's. "I was dead once. Technically speaking."

"Technically speaking?" Keane echoed.

"I was running the engine room on a UBC freighter a while back. During a supply run through the Nosch Sector we got blindsided by Enki raiders. Their first shots took out our weapons. I had to manually reboot the entire system. During the process I got caught between two deuterium generators as they fired up simultaneously. Burned off every hair on my body for nearly a year and stopped my heart for ten whole seconds." Warrick's lips wrinkled under his thick beard. "I'm not a doctor, but I'm pretty sure that meant I was dead."

Keane held up his left hand. "This hand was ripped from my body and I had been invaded by an alien entity that was consuming not only my body, but I think my soul."

Warrick pounded his chest and burped. "I don't think it's a damn contest."

"Sure, sure," Keane agreed. "But I'm kind of bothered by one particular thing."

"The fact that an all-powerful alien being restored you completely?" Warrick asked.

Keane shook his head. "No."

Warrick looked over Keane at Nax and raised his eyebrows. "It's what I would be worried about."

"I'm not having any nightmares." Keane rested his chin on the table, staring through the empty glasses at the Fauliran dancers that gyrated atop the Daboo tables. Their tails swished back and forth, lashing against faces of men who couldn't decide if their fortunes were going up or down. "You'd think I'd be having some nightmares. Right? It's the sort of traumatic incident that results in nightmares." He looked at Warrick. "You had dreams about being dead for those ten seconds?"

Warrick's face scrunched up as he took a moment to remember. "Sure, I guess. Maybe a couple of restless nights. Mostly I was bothered by the fact that I looked like a hairless Fim'ai shit weasel for the next year."

"I sleep like a damn baby," Keane said.

"Babies don't get any damn sleep," Warrick said. "They wake up every four hours. Hell, that's just human babies. Stravin babies? Well, shit, they don't get any sleep for the first two years."

Keane looked at him. "How is that something you know?"

Warrick puffed out his chest. "I'll have you know, I was in a long-term relationship with a delightful Stravin single mother." He paused and then added, "Well, she was delightful. Her brood was a damn nightmare. I'm pretty sure I hate kids now."

"Kids," Keane murmured. He straightened up. "I wonder if I can even have kids now. I couldn't before." He looked down at his torso and tapped his lower abdomen. "The accident on Serenity Base left me unable to produce viable sperm."

An uncomfortable look passed across Warrick's face.

Keane shrugged. "I'm just telling you what the doctors told me."

"I don't know if I want to know what the doctors told you," Warrick replied.

"I don't think I wanted to know either," Keane admitted. "But there it was. And now? How am I supposed to ask Marlize or the old bastard to check and see if I'm producing viable sperm?"

"Ya don't," Warrick said. "You just live with the mystery of it all like the rest of us."

"I just don't think I'm supposed to be this well-adjusted after something like this," Keane said.

"I don't know that I would call you well-adjusted," Warrick said. "Well-adjusted people don't talk about whether or not they have viable sperm."

Keane looked at Nax. "What about you, Nax? What do you think?"

"I don't think Jaxson's wrong," Nax said. "Even on Natuzzi it's considered bad form to discuss one's reproductive abilities."

"You know, Nax, nobody gives you enough credit for being funny," Keane said dryly.

"It's my constant burden," Nax replied. "I also think that you experienced something unique to you. There's nobody to tell you what the right or wrong way to react to it is, because nobody else has experienced it."

"So nothing I'm feeling is wrong?"

"Of course, it could also mean nothing you're feeling is right, either," Nax said.

Keane frowned. "That's not very helpful either."

Nax shrugged. "I don't have experience with limbs being ripped from my body and then magically restored."

"Well, I'm pretty sure it wasn't magic," Keane said.

"I'm not," Warrick said. "I'm not a doctor, but the human body isn't all that different from any other machine and there are some things you just can't get original parts for." He reached over and poked Keane's left hand. "That looks pretty damn original to me. If that's not magic, then what is it?"

"Just a form of science we don't understand yet," Keane said, bristling slightly.

"Bullshit."

"You're supposed to be an engineer," Keane said. "Science, facts. Part A goes into Part B."

"Well, first, that sounds like a pretty damn condescending description of what I do," Warrick said. "Second, there's just some shit out there that doesn't make any sense."

"He's not wrong," Nax agreed. "Every two hundredth

Asron born has an ability to perceive gamma rays. There's nothing in their biology that suggests such a thing is possible and when examined, there's nothing present in the individual that explains this ability."

"Magic," Warrick whispered.

"I don't believe in magic," Keane said, a sour tone in his voice.

"I don't think you need to believe in it for it to work," Nax said.

Keane smacked his hands on the table and pushed himself to his feet. "Well, screw that."

"I once had sex with a Backlon death witch," Warrick said. "I'm not sure if she was magic, but she sure as hell did things to my body that were magical."

"As I recall, she also gave you a raging case of Type C Backlon herpes," Nax said.

Warrick shrugged. "Well, sure, no relationship is perfect."

"I need more alcohol." Keane turned in a half circle, looking for the bar. "I'm not drunk enough to contemplate the nature of my existence without suffering crippling depression."

Warrick held up an empty glass. "Amen to that, brother."

"I say whoever hasn't had a near-death experience buys the next round."

Both men turned to Nax, who sighed and got to his feet.

6
_____

HAWKINS FELL in step beside him as Nax got up from the table. She didn't say anything as he navigated his way through the main floor of Dreks Tavern. Her hands were clasped behind her back and there was a bounce in her step. This was the first time he had seen her in something other than her Fleet uniform. The dress was similar to the one she had worn on their first date: An almost skintight red bodice that transformed just above the waist into wide, flowing skirt that all but demanded her to twirl around. The difference this time was the length of the skirt. That night, it had gone just below her knees. Now, however, it sat almost nine inches above her knees and with every step she took, every twirl and bounce threatened to expose an indecent amount of milky white flesh that normally wasn't exposed outside of the bedroom.

It didn't go unnoticed by Nax, despite his every best effort.

"This is nice," she said as they reached the bar.

Nax took stock of who might be around him before answering. This corner of the bar was empty, which was unfortunate as the bartender felt no need to acknowledge Nax's presence.

"What is?" he replied finally.

"This." Hawkins gestured with her hand at the bar and then back towards the table where they had left Warrick and Keane. "Guy's night out. You know, I don't think I remember you ever having a guy's night out before."

"Jaxson and I spend plenty of social time together," Nax said, trying to catch the eye of the bartender.

"Yeah, sure." Hawkins took a seat on one of the empty stools, resting her elbows on the bar. "But you and Warrick are like brothers. That's hardly a guy's night out. And, to be fair, this isn't much of a guy's night out either. You really should have tried to rope in Zemble."

"He doesn't care for social drinking."

She nodded. "Yeah, I guess." Her eyes lit up abruptly. "Oh! You know who you should have brought with you? The Old Bastard."

Nax looked at her. "Doctor Rabkin?"

"Well, I'm not talking about my dad," Hawkins said. "He's been dead for fifteen years and I don't think he would have liked you very much."

Nax went back to trying to catch the attention of the bartender. "I don't think Doctor Rabkin is the..." he paused for a second, "*vibe* Keane was going for."

Hawkins shrugged, spinning around on the stool. "Oh, I don't know about that. I always thought he'd be a fun guy to get drunk with."

"Did you?"

"Yup."

"Because it's not something I've ever considered."

"Which is why I said that it was something I have."

Nax looked at her again. "Except that you're not real?"

Hawkins stopped spinning in her chair. "I'm sorry? Are we back to this again?"

"We never left it."

"Of course I'm real. You're talking to me."

"And your assumption is that I would never talk to someone that wasn't real?"

"Well, I guess that depends on what you consider to be real," Hawkins said.

Nax turned away from her again, but didn't bother trying to flag down the bartender.

"Or maybe it hinges more on whether or not it matters if I'm real or not," she added.

Nax didn't respond to that either.

She hopped off the stool and twirled. The hem of her skirt nearly flew up to her waist. "You haven't said anything about my dress."

"It's beautiful."

"I wore it just for you," she said. "You know what it reminds me of?"

A bittersweet smile passed across Nax's face. "Our first date."

Hawkins smiled. It was bright, charming and a little naughty. "You know, it's going to be our anniversary in a few weeks."

"I hadn't forgotten."

The smile drifted from her face as she pressed her skirt down. "No, but you were trying to."

"To be fair," he said, "I'm not entirely certain how I'm supposed to celebrate this year."

"I was thinking of just a small, intimate dinner," she replied.

"Just the two of us?"

"Well, we can invite some friends. But I don't think any

of them are really going to want to talk to me." When Nax didn't smile or laugh, she added, "That was supposed to be a joke."

"I know," he said. "I just didn't think it was very funny."

"You're clearly in a mood and nothing I say is going to change it, is it?"

"I'm not in a mood," Nax replied. "I'm having a delightful night."

"You could just tell him."

Nax just stared at her like he didn't know what she was talking about.

"Oh, please." Hawkins rolled her eyes. "Don't pretend like you don't know what I'm talking about."

Nax took a deep breath and exhaled through his nose slowly. "I've talked to Warrick."

"No. You should *talk* to him."

"I fail to see the difference between what I said and what you're saying."

"Yes you do. You're just playing stupid and that doesn't really work when the person you're talking to is occupying the same headspace as you."

"I can't talk to Jaxson about you."

"Sure you can."

"He's made his position very clear."

"Based on limited facts."

"It's not as if I have anything more to share with him."

"That's not true."

"As you already pointed out, he's probably not going to want to speak with you."

"Why are we fighting about this?"

Nax shrugged. "I genuinely don't know."

"You could use a friend," Hawkins said. "Somebody who'll be on your side."

"Isn't that what you're supposed to be?"

"Well, I'm not going to be much of a character witness if it comes down to that."

"Is that what it's going to come down to?"

"If you don't talk to Warrick. Maybe?"

"I'm not crazy."

"I didn't say you were."

"That would hold more weight if you weren't a voice in my head."

She held out her arms and did a little twirl. "I'd say this is more than just a voice in your head."

Nax didn't know what to say to that.

Hawkins sighed. "The universe is a strange and magnificent place. There are going to be things that don't make any sense."

"And what if this isn't one of those things?"

Hawkins smiled impishly. "I'm no expert, but this feels pretty magical, doesn't it?"

"There's a thin line between magic and madness."

"I'll concede to that," she said. "But what good is it going to do for you to find out what side you fall on? At the end of the day, I'm still dead and you're still talking to a ghost in your mind."

Nax sighed, rubbing his eyes. "Grace..."

"I like to think that maybe we're somewhere in the middle," she continued. "That it's a little bit of both. Because that's where the real magic lies, you know. A little bit of column A and a little bit of column B. The measurements are never the same, of course. This means that it never mixes quite the same for everybody. Keeps things *special*."

"That doesn't sound like something I'd say," Nax replied.

Hawkins arched an eyebrow. "Are you sure about that?

Because we tend to sound different when our words are coming out of somebody else's mouth."

Nax turned away from her, leaning against the bar. "If I'm losing my mind..." His voice was barely louder than a whisper.

Hawkins leaned in, wrapping an arm around him. "There are worse ways to go."

He closed his eyes, trying to remember what it felt like for her to touch him and found that this moment felt far more real than it had any right to. "Grace..." he whispered.

"Maybe it's nothing at all," she whispered back.

"Maybe."

"Maybe it's just a dream."

"Then maybe I don't want to wake up."

"Neither would I."

He opened his eyes and turned to look at her, but she was already gone.

7

IN HIS YOUNGER DAYS, Ambassador Caldwell Reynoso had charm and looks to spare. He had been notable for maintaining affairs with the wives of various heads of state, based solely on the square line of his jaw and the quick wit of his tongue. No one was attracted to him because he had power, at the time he had simply been a lowly aide to Monroe Hansma. It was his pure *presence*. The charm that practically oozed from his pores, mixed with the classical looks of a celebrity from a bygone era, transformed Caldwell Reynoso from a mere faceless underling to a man who generated his own gravitational pull wherever he went.

But Ambassador Reynoso's younger days were long behind him.

Today the only thing he had absolute control over was how quickly he could finish off a bottle of Soveer ale and even that was less than impressive.

Leaning against the wall in the quiet corridor of the *Atlantic* he stared down at the bottle of purple liquid in his hand, struggling between confusion and surprise at why it was still over half full. Clearly, he was slipping in his old age.

A bottle this size? He should have polished it off...Well, whenever it was when he started it.

His face bunched up as he tried to remember just exactly how long he had been nursing this particular bottle and was irritated to discover he couldn't even recall opening it.

Like his looks, his memory was transforming into something that was nothing more than a faint, unimpressive echo of what it used to be.

"Or," Reynoso muttered out loud, stroking the double chin that had taken over his square jaw. "Maybe I didn't open the bottle in the first place and that's why I can't remember?"

He looked around the empty corridor, as if to find somebody who might agree with him. But for most of the residents of the Atlantic it was the middle of the night and so the good ambassador was in short supply of yes men.

Reynoso shrugged and turned his attention back to his bottle, deciding that he didn't need any outside validation for this one. It seemed pretty obvious he was in the right anyway. But just to put a bow on it, he said out loud, "Sounds pretty plausible to me," and then took a long swig from the bottle.

He patted down his wrinkled uniform in a vague attempt to make sure he hadn't spilled any of the exotic and, more importantly, *expensive* liquor. He was dry, more or less. Unflattering patches of sweat were littered under his arms and around his expanded gut. He took a long, deep breath, which, in of itself, was a strenuous effort. He wiped at his mouth with the back of his sleeve as he tried to remember what had prompted him to hike all the way down to the *Atlantic's* lower decks in the first place.

At first, like the mystery of the slowly draining bottle of

Soveer, Reynoso came up with an empty fog of nothingness. This happened more often than he cared to admit.

It wasn't his fault, of course. It was this damn *assignment*. Nearly a decade he had been out here on the *Atlantic* in his position as the UPA's Ambassador to the Veneer Empire. At any other time in history, it would have been a position of great esteem. But at this particular time in history, it was a dead-end job. Because no one had heard from the Veneer Empire in over a hundred years. Not a peep. Not a word. Not a stray transmission. The Veneer Empire had simply closed up all the doors, drew the curtains and turned off all the comms.

So what was there for him to do? Nothing. There was no one to liaison with. There was nothing to negotiate. There were no relationships to finesse. Ambassador Caldwell Reynoso was there 'just in case.'

It was a place they sent undesirables who could no longer behave themselves within the upper echelons of the UPA. It was a position they gave to ambassadors who couldn't be bothered to exercise any decorum.

Reynoso sighed loudly.

There just wasn't a damn thing for him to do out here in the middle of nowhere, except get drunk and gamble. He couldn't even touch any of Kosan's girls anymore. Not after what happened the last time. Which, he had contended was not his fault. And besides, he was a paying customer. And what was that old adage? The customer is always right?

Twenty years ago Caldwell Reynoso could have had any woman he wanted and he did.

Now he couldn't even pay for a damn prostitute.

He raised the bottle to his lips again, but didn't tip it forward enough for anything to make it out. He didn't notice though. Reynoso's eyes had glazed over with regret and shame and all he could really see at the moment was a series of ill-timed choices from his past that had led him to this particular moment.

And then he remembered what he was doing down here in the first place.

Bendare.

Right.

Reynoso took another pull from the bottle. This one shorter, but he didn't notice. His mind was elsewhere again.

He started walking again, his feet shuffling every few steps as the expensive liquor slowly settled into his body.

Bendare had sent him a message through Fizza. Wanted to meet him down on the lower ring. It couldn't have been for anything good, of course. At least not in Fizza's opinion, which he loudly stated despite Reynoso's insistence that he not. Reynoso coughed, remembering when he was an aide to Ambassador Hansma. He knew the fine art of keeping his mouth shut. Because when he didn't, Hansma would just knock him up the backside of his head. Of course, Reynoso got the last laugh since he spent most of his appointment having more sex with the ambassador's wife than the ambassador did. Reynoso smiled at the memory of sleeping with Hansma's wife like the dirty old man he was.

Fizza had insisted that there was nothing worth doing on the lower ring after midnight, local time. Unless, of course, you were looking to score something along the lines of drugs, prostitutes or some exotic alcohol that the UPA had an embargo against. Reynoso had said he was hoping for a lead on a whore house, but he'd be more than happy with either of the other two.

Except...

Except that it had been months since he heard from Bendare. Reynoso had forgotten the Chirotian was even still around. He just assumed that Commodore Straub had finally gotten wise to her and sent Bendare packing.

Clearly, though, she hadn't. And now here he was wandering the dark, empty corridors looking for his favorite Chirot opium supplier who he was almost certain wasn't interested in selling to Reynoso, not after what happened last time.

"Son of a bitch," Reynoso muttered. He stopped at a Y junction, trying to remember which way he was supposed to go. The situation became worse as his eyes started to insist that there were *two* Y junctions. "Shoulda just had the purple bitch come up to my office."

He rubbed his eyes, laughing at the conniption fit Fizza would have if Bendare had just walked down the corridors of B Deck and strolled right into the office of one Ambassador Caldwell Reynoso. But, really, what would they have done? His life was already basically a living hell. Were they going to strip Reynoso of his title and send him back to Earth? Because if anybody asked him, that sounded like a pretty damn good idea right about now.

Reynoso's laughter turned into a coughing fit that he tried to quell with a large swallow of the Soveer ale. The coughing subsided, eventually, but the two Y junctions were still there. He rubbed his eyes again and squinted until they slowly resolved back into one.

Okay. One problem solved. More or less.

There was a dull pounding taking shape at the top of his forehead and slowly radiating back.

"Son of a bitch," he muttered again and flipped a mental coin. The left corridor came up heads, but instead he decided to go right based on a fuzzy memory that was over a year old.

Reynoso stumbled down the corridor, unaware of the

noise the glass bottle made as it clanked against the wall every time he lost his balance, which was really all the time. It was remarkable that he didn't notice it, considering it was the only noise in the otherwise quiet corridor. Every time the bottle struck the wall it echoed in front and behind him. This was a mostly unoccupied section of the *Atlantic*. Anyone who maintained a residence down here did so because they were hiding and therefore weren't inclined to check on what might be making an annoying clanking noise in the corridor.

After almost another fifteen minutes stumbling around, which in Reynoso's booze-addled mind felt more like an hour, the ambassador finally just stopped and admitted to himself that he was lost.

Reynoso checked the bottle of Soveer ale. It still wasn't empty. How had he not managed to finish the damn thing off yet?

He turned in a half circle, trying to remember which direction he had just come from, when there was a voice over his shoulder.

Reynoso turned again and found two hazy forms standing behind him. Remembering what happened earlier at the Y junction he squinted and the hazy forms merged into one familiar figure.

The ambassador smiled and opened his mouth to say, "What the hell are you doing down here?" But he didn't get past the first word before everything went black.

8

"GENTLEMEN, I'm going to be honest with you: I want your business. I really, truly do. I love UPA Fleet officers. You spend so much time zipping around the galaxy, you don't have any time to spend your money, so you've got *plenty* of it to spend. And I love it when you come to spend it in my establishment. So right up front, I need you to understand: your money is very, very, *very* good here. So it's not about the money. It's about making sure you're going to keep coming back here to spend your money. And this drink? This is not the kind of drink that's going to bring you back to my fine establishment. That's not to say that I am ashamed of this drink. Far from it. This is a *fine* drink. One of the best drinks on the menu. In fact, this drink is only available in six locations. That means there's only five other locations that are even *licensed* to carry this drink. So not only is this a fine drink, the best drink on my menu, but it is the most *elite* drink. Mind you, it's not the most expensive. That would be the Soveer ale and I would love to sell you a shot glass of that, but we all know none of you can afford it and that's fine.

But this drink here? Sure you can afford it, but that doesn't mean you should drink it. You drink this? I can almost guarantee you'll never come back here. Either because you'll end up dead, which happens to less than ten percent of the people who try this amazing beverage or you'll end up psychologically scarred from the experience on a level that even walking by my establishment will trigger some kind of severe nervous breakdown. And that's not good for you, it's not good for my business, and it's not good for me. So please, with the utmost respect I say this, pick another drink."

Keane and Warrick sat on the opposite side of the bar, listening with intense concentration to Dreks' every word. The proprietor of Dreks Tavern was a squat figure with an almost block-like head and wide, oval-shaped eyes that seemed to focus on everything all at once. Like most Krumixes his age his green skin was covered in dark purple spots that seemed to shift and move under the dim lighting of the bar. He didn't look like the kind of individual who had an extensive vocabulary and new patrons, and old patrons who were too drunk to remember, were constantly surprised by his verbosity

Behind Keane and Warrick the din of the late-night regulars was almost drowned out by Dreks' hypnotic-like speech and, for the briefest of moments, both men forgot where they even were.

Everything was about this *drink*.

This magnificent beverage they had heard only whispered rumors of.

Proog Doldoss' Blitz Delight

Keane and Warrick were speechless.

The background noise of the bar slowly rolled its way back over them, bringing them back to the here and now.

They looked at each other. A wordless message passed between them. They both turned back to Dreks.

"Well?" Dreks asked.

"That was a hell of a sales pitch," Keane said.

"Amen to that," Warrick agreed.

"Truly a thing of beauty," Keane added.

From the other side of Keane Nax raised a hairless eyebrow. "Perhaps I heard something different?"

Keane held up two fingers. "I'll take two of Proog Doldoss' Blitz Delight."

Warrick grinned. "As will I."

They both looked at Nax.

Nax frowned. "I'll be heeding the bartender's warning."

"*Warning*?" Keane repeated. "That was no *warning*. This is possibly the greatest drink I've ever heard of. And I once spent a weekend on Tilden's Moon where you could get Boveran Blood wine. Have you ever tried Boveran blood wine? It's liquid joy distilled down for consumption by the unclean masses. This?" he pointed in the direction of where Dreks had disappeared to get their drinks. "Sounds like it's going to make Boveran blood wine taste like Boveran dogs' shit."

"Assuming you survive the experience," Nax said.

"Of course," Keane said. "That's clearly what makes it a superior drink. If I die tonight, I can't think of a better way to go."

Warrick lifted his half empty glass of Backlon whiskey. "Amen to that."

"Perhaps we should consider less alcohol at this point," Nax suggested. "Since I don't believe there's anything in this particular beverage that's going to help your physical or mental state."

Keane looked at him like he had suddenly started

ranting about how the entirety of the universe was contained in a single marble no bigger than the tip of his pinky. "Are you out of your damn mind?"

Warrick raised a finger. "As a matter of fact, he *is* out of his damn mind."

"I'm sorry?" Keane asked, looking back and forth between them.

Nax regarded Warrick coolly. "You are extremely inebriated."

Warrick's mouth wrinkled and then he burped. "Well, sure. That doesn't change the fact that you're stone-cold sober and you're talking to your dead girlfriend."

Keane raised both of his eyebrows and wiggled. "Oh, that sounds like a story. I want to hear more about this. I love hearing stories about people talking to their dead lovers."

Warrick looked at Keane with a puzzled expression. "Say what now?"

"This doesn't happen to you when you go out drinking?" Keane asked. "It happens to me all the time. Especially if there's some dodgy Backlon alcohol involved. That shit brings up some serious, deep-seated issues every time."

Warrick nodded. "Except this isn't that. He's one hundred percent sober when he's talking to Grace."

Keane turned back to Nax. "This definitely sounds like a story I need to hear."

"There's no story to tell," Nax said, maintaining a neutral expression.

Warrick leaned across Keane to poke at Nax. "That's because he's not allowed to tell anybody who's not a Natuzzi. Apparently neither am I. But I don't really care anymore and that's not just the six shots of Backlon whiskey talking."

Nax made a clicking sound with his tongue against the roof of his mouth.

"I changed my mind." Keane rubbed his face. "This is starting to feel uncomfortably like an actual thing that I am definitely not drunk enough to be a part of."

"Well, it's a matter of security," Warrick said. His words were starting to slur together a little. "Right? Ship's pilot is hallucinating? That's a problem, right? It's got to be some kind of a security issue."

"Except that I'm not and it's not," Nax said. "You're drunk."

"And yet," Warrick burped again, "I've got it more together than you right now because I'm not hallucinating my dead girlfriend."

Nax's fingers flexed into a fist on the surface of the bar. It did not go unnoticed by Keane.

"Okay, this is getting dangerously close to me having to pull the plug on guy's night here and I don't think any of us are in a position to be having a meeting with Captain Mitchell about anything right now. So why don't we just table whatever this is until we're all sober? That sound like a good idea?"

Warrick made a face and pointed at Nax. "You're going to get somebody killed. Worse, you're going to get *yourself* killed."

"I think Commander Keane has made a valid point," Nax replied. His voice was starting to sound a little strained.

"Oh boy," Keane muttered. "Now you're referring to me by rank. This is actually getting worse. Okay." He held up both hands. "Okay."

"I have no problem with terminating this conversation," Nax said.

"Sure you don't," Warrick said. "Because if nobody else knows about it, you don't have to do anything about it."

"Jaxson," Nax began, a warning tone in his voice.

Dreks came back with a tray of four shot glasses and a small lizard-like creature in a tiny cage.

"Oh, thank goodness." Keane clapped his hands together. "More alcohol to distract us."

The creature in the cage was about a foot long. Its head was almost flat and ended in sharp edges, creating a triangular appearance. It twitched side to side as it lazily circled its small cage, staring up at Keane and Warrick with the disinterest of a creature that just couldn't be bothered to care. Its skin had a translucent quality and as it moved around its small cage brief glimpses of its internal organs could be seen. On its back and going down its tail were tiny blue orbs that had a chalky texture to them and appeared to roll slightly as the creature moved, but never seemed in danger of falling off.

Next to the creature's cage were four empty shot glasses and four lime slices.

Warrick rubbed his eyes and then pointed at the empty glasses. "I know that I'm already a bit buzzed here, but are those empty? Where's the damn drink?"

A crack appeared in the lower half of Dreks' face. It was a wide, yawning chasm that made Warrick afraid that the man's face was about to fall apart. Then the alcohol-fueled haze in his mind cleared up and he realized Dreks was just smiling.

"As you humans say: some assembly required," Dreks replied.

Keane's head bobbed up and down as he rapped his palms against the surface of the bar. "Okay, okay. I'm still onboard. What do we need to do?"

Dreks pointed to the creature in the cage. "This here is the titular Proog Doldoss in the Proog Doldoss' Blitz Delight. She can produce up to six ounces of Bliz Delight every hour."

"Produce?" Warrick echoed.

"You'll need to extract it from her adrenal glands," Dreks continued. He pointed to the chalky blue bulbs that trailed along its back. "That's what those are." He held up his left hand and curled his blocky fingers in towards each other. "You're going to want to hold the Doldoss like so in one hand, positioning her over your glass and with your other hand," he took his forefinger and thumb from his right hand and hovered them over his left hand, "you're going to gently massage each orb until you get your desired amount of Delight in your glass. Now, the trick, of course, is to not let her bite you while you do this."

"Is this a painful experience for the creature?" Nax asked.

"Actually, no," Dress replied. "It's rather quite pleasurable for the Doldoss. In her insect-sized brain, she interprets the entire procedure as a form of foreplay. Proog Doldoss' routinely bite at each other during mating season, sometimes even killing each other in the throes of passion. They're actually a protected species because of this. After all, the whole point of banging around with a member of the opposite sex is to reproduce." He nodded at the Doldoss in the cage. "These little beauties are too stupid to realize that. Killing each other during the process kind of defeats the purpose."

Keane looked at Warrick. "Well?"

Warrick scratched his beard. "I'm not going to lie. I've done some weird shit before, but this is new. Does it hurt?"

"When she bites you? Feels like a ten-pound Seexoar cat

trying to rip off your hand," Dreks replied. "That's because of her saliva, which has a hallucinogenic-like reaction in most species. Especially humans. If you were another Doldoss, of course, it acts like a damn aphrodisiac, which helps get the male member of the species even more wound up. The only species not known to have a reaction to her saliva is the Elwat."

"I definitely should have invited Zemble," Keane muttered.

The bartender rubbed his hands together. "So, what do we say gentlemen? Are we still on board?"

Keane looked at Warrick again.

"Honestly? I feel like I've come too far at this point," Warrick said. "Can't turn back now."

Keane grinned. "My thoughts exactly." He turned back to Dreks. "Let's do this."

Dreks nodded and pulled out a datapad from underneath his bar. "Alright then. Now, before we get started, I've got just a few releases that I'm legally required to have you sign."

9

"HOW RELIABLE IS THIS INTEL?"

On the screen Admiral Philip Wanamaker didn't answer right away. Instead he made a face that didn't inspire a lot of confidence.

Captain Gavin Mitchell pushed back from the table, exasperated. He ran his hands through his salt and pepper hair. "What the hell, Phil?"

The conference room was small to the point of being almost claustrophobic. The screen that Wanamaker was projected on took up too much space at the far end of the room, making it seem even smaller.

Wanamaker took a deep breath before answering. "It's as reliable as we're going to get right now."

Mitchell glanced at the woman on the opposite end of the table. Commodore Kathryn Straub leaned forward in her chair, one hand propped up on the table, holding the side of her head up. The collar of her uniform was unzipped down to just under her collarbone and her sleeves were rolled up. She had a weariness to her that suggested she hadn't had more than a couple of hours of sleep in the last several weeks. She returned Mitchell's look with a half shrug.

"I saw that," Wanamaker growled.

"Good," Mitchell replied, jabbing his finger in Wanamaker's direction. "I wanted you to see it and realize the two senior officers you still have active in Directive Fifty-Two don't exactly have a lot of confidence in your intel right now."

Wanamaker grunted. "Hell, I don't have a lot of confidence either. Over half of the Veneer Empire has just gone dark and I'm not particularly eager to send anybody in there to find out why."

Mitchell held up his hands. "Then where are we getting our intel from?"

Wanamaker cleared his throat. "A reliable source."

"*Reliable*?" Mitchell echoed with disbelief.

"You want me to dig up the definition of the word?" Wanamaker asked. "Something about it is clearly making you confused."

"I don't think it's so much the word as it is *who's* saying it," Mitchell replied.

Wanamaker frowned. "Suddenly you're having difficulty accepting information from your superior officer?"

"Only because my superior officer has spent the last month bouncing around the Alliance in an effort to avoid getting arrested by the President of the UPA."

"He's not going to arrest me," Wanamaker said. "At least, not officially. And seeing as how I've made a career out of unofficially detaining people; I'm not looking forward to being on the receiving end of that."

"But President D'Ambra doesn't believe in those kinds of blackhat operations," Straub said with obviously faux naiveté in her voice.

Wanamaker scoffed. "Of course not. This is a *transparent* administration. That's why he waited until *afterwards* to notify the public about the drone strikes on Giana Prime. So, sure, maybe he won't snatch me up in the middle of the night. But he'll sure as hell string me up as a damn straw man for whatever piece of shit security legislation he wants to get passed." Wanamaker took a deep calming breath to keep himself from getting any further worked up. "Look, I'll be the first to tell you it's a shaggy setup. But this is the closest we're going to get to receiving actual intel out of Veneer space without actually sending somebody in there."

Straub sat up. "Wait a minute, this is the second time you've said something to that effect. Where's your intel source located?"

"Well, he's certainly not in Veneer space if you haven't picked up on it yet," Wanamaker said.

"Damnit, Phil," Mitchell muttered.

"Then where is he?" Straub said.

"A quaint little location I like to call 'Top Secret, Highly Classified.'"

"Last time I checked, our security clearances went to the top," Mitchell said.

"That they do," Wanamaker agreed. "Doesn't mean I'm going to tell you where my asset is. Less people know, the better. Hell, *I* don't even want to know." He leaned forward until his face filled the screen. "Look, none of us are happy about this. Me, least of all. I'm trying to protect half the galaxy with both hands tied behind my back. If I wanted to perform magic tricks, I wouldn't have gotten into the Fleet."

"You'd be a terrible magician," Mitchell said. "I can't remember the last time you successfully disappeared."

Wanamaker grunted again with a half-smile. He leaned back. "Look, here's what we know: the Unity and the Veneer had an alliance. That alliance most likely resulted in the destruction of, at the very least, the Veneer government, if not their entire damn home world. Do you know what the population of the Veneer home world was the last time we had a count of it?"

Neither Mitchell or Straub replied.

"One hundred years ago it was over ten billion. People who are better with math than I am extrapolated their current number at four times that." Wanamaker folded his arms. "The *entire planet* has gone silent. Not a single transmission coming out of it. We've pinged some of the Veneer colonies, the ones that we know are still alive, and they're just as confused as us. The difference, of course, is that they can send a ship there to investigate without starting an interstellar conflict."

"But nobody's sending any ships that way," Mitchell said.

"No, they are not," Wanamaker said.

"And your intel source would have us believe that's because of the Oxean Syndicate," Straub said.

"It's not the craziest idea I've heard this week," Wanamaker.

Mitchell stroked his chin. "Except that the Syndicate isn't interested in governing. They're basically a large-scale crime family."

"Sure, but I wouldn't call what the Syndicate is doing 'governing,'" Wanamaker said. "It's more like taking hold of a wounded animal and keeping it from healing properly. Or, worse, letting it heal and then breaking its other leg."

"Damnit," Mitchell said.

"Here's the thing," Wanamaker said. "We all know that one way or another D'Ambra wants the Veneer Empire back in the UPA. Hell, according to an aide one of my former lieutenants is dating, he's building his damn reelection campaign around it. Of course, it's hard to open talks with an empire that doesn't exist anymore. But if there was another power in play in the same region of space…"

Mitchell's face darkened as he understood the implication. "You can't be serious."

"I'm dead serious," Wanamaker replied. "You don't have to take this with a grain of salt because D'Ambra's been hounding the new Security Council for intel to start talks with the Oxeans."

Mitchell shook his head. "The Oxeans are-"

"-about to be, essentially, the governing power in one of the largest sectors of space within the vicinity of UPA borders," Wanamaker said. "With access to those sectors again we can cut weeks, hell *months*, off travel times. Suddenly, the outer rim is just the next-door rim. Never mind all the resources the Alliance can start exploiting again. Or has everybody forgotten that the Veneer have the largest supply of ombrium for terraforming by a considerable margin?"

"He can't possibly think he can actually negotiate with the *Oxean Syndicate*?" Mitchell asked. "They're a terrorist organization."

"Not according to the Security Council," Wanamaker reminded.

"Because it seems like we shouldn't have to classify something that's obvious to literally everybody else in the damn galaxy," Mitchell said.

"Sure, you think that. I think that," Wanamaker said. "But apparently common sense has taken its leave of the current administration. And as such, since the Oxean Syndicate isn't technically categorized as a terrorist organization, the President of the United Planetary Alliance can comfortably enter negotiations with them about becoming valued members of the UPA." Wanamaker held out his hands, palms up. "That's how politics work."

"The minute he steps into that room they'll shoot him just as soon as look at him," Mitchell said.

"You're assuming the Syndicate isn't going to be interested in making a deal," Wanamaker said.

"What could they possibly get that they wouldn't be bothered to just steal or murder for in the first place?" Straub asked.

"Legitimacy," Wanamaker said. "After all, if they're a member of the UPA, they can't be all that bad, can they? Or, to put it more bluntly: if they're part of the law, then their actions can't be considered breaking the law."

Mitchell got up from the table, suddenly feeling the claustrophobia of the room. "Son of a bitch."

"Yeah, it's all pretty shitty news," Wanamaker said.

"Which brings us back to my original question," Mitchell said. "How reliable is your source?"

"Considering what I'm hearing through the grapevine about D'Ambra's political aspirations? I think my source is on the damn money."

"What about the remaining Veneer?" Straub asked. "They've got to have some say in this?"

"Either there's too few of them to confidently confront the Syndicate or they're focused on the very real possibility of their own extinction. Either way, my source says they're not a part of the conversation."

"That's gonna come back and bite somebody in the ass," Mitchell said.

"Fingers crossed it's the Oxeans and not us," Wanamaker replied.

"Amen to that," Straub agreed.

"So what are we supposed to do with this intel from your reliable source?" Mitchell asked.

"Nothing," Wanamaker said.

Straub rubbed her face. "That's a hell of a punchline."

"Directive Fifty-Two still needs to stay under the radar. Your ship is the one resource I do have and it's not going anywhere any time soon. So right now, you do nothing."

"Then what the hell is this?" Mitchell asked.

"This is me keeping you in the loop so you don't get caught with your pants down around your ankles," Wanamaker said. "When shit goes south in the Neutral Zone because the Oxeans decided to renege on whatever treaty D'Ambra gets them to sign, you're going to be the first to feel it."

"And here I was, worried I wouldn't have anything to look forward to what with the last threat to galactic peace taken off the board," Straub said flatly.

"I don't like that plan," Mitchell growled.

"I like it even less," Wanamaker said. "It's not like D'Ambra or the Oxeans are going to sit around and wait for us to get caught up."

"So we just scramble like chickens with their heads cut off, hoping that things don't get worse?" Mitchell asked.

"What about your source?" Straub asked. "He's an active asset? Can we use him?"

Wanamaker sighed. "Not without causing a completely different interstellar incident. Right now he's so deep undercover his own mother wouldn't recognize him. Hell, I don't even have a direct line to him. The only way we got this was through a dead drop out on the Ahines comet. And then, to top it off, we don't have any actual extraction plan in place, so he's basically stuck behind enemy lines."

"You know, it's amazing to me that we're supposed to be

the professionals around here," Straub said. "How do you send somebody in without a damn extraction plan?"

"Very carefully," Wanamaker said. "After all, we didn't have an extraction plan in place so we couldn't afford to have everything blow up on day one."

"I don't like the sound of that, Phil," Mitchell said.

"Yeah, well, join the damn club." Wanamaker took a deep breath and slowly exhaled. "It's a real shitshow out here, Gavin. I put out one supernova and six more pop up to take its place. Everywhere I turn it looks like the damn galaxy is falling apart."

"It's always possible we could still get lucky," Straub said.

"Oh? And how's that?" Wanamaker asked.

She shrugged. "Maybe the Oxean representative just shoots D'Ambra the minute he steps into the room."

Wanamaker shook his head. "I'm going to sign off before you get me implicated on charges of treason." He looked at Mitchell. "Keep a low profile until you hear back from me. Your new XO should be there any day now and I don't want a report on my desk about how he found you unfit for command on his first day there."

Mitchell just shrugged wordlessly.

Wanamaker disappeared from the screen.

Neither of them spoke, staring at the blank screen for several moments.

"Shit," Straub muttered finally, rubbing her face.

"What?" Mitchell asked.

She got to her feet. "Reynoso's already a drunken pain in my ass now and he doesn't have anything to do. What kind of drunken pain in the ass is he going to be when he finds out his position is obsolete and he's being left out of the biggest peace talk of his career?"

Mitchell grunted. "Peace talk. Sure."

Straub followed him out the door into the main corridor of C deck.

"What the hell else am I supposed to call it?"

"Shitshow has a nice ring to it."

"Sure." Straub nodded. "That'd look good in a report, too. Spice things up a bit."

"Konheim used to file profanity-ladened reports all the time," Mitchell said. "They eventually made him an admiral."

"Because they wanted him to stop filing all those reports."

Mitchell shrugged. "Failing upwards is still going up."

She shook her head. "Maybe I'll get lucky and Reynoso'll drink himself to death before he hears about this."

"Your definition of 'lucky' is starting to concern me," Mitchell said as they made their way down the corridor.

"Well, if it's a bad thing for somebody else that results in good fortune for me, it still counts as being lucky."

"It sounds like you're trying to throw my words back at me."

"Good. Then it's working." They rounded a corner. "My engineers say your ship's never going to be space worthy again." There was a playful smirk tugging at the corners of her mouth as she waited for a response.

Mitchell looked at her from the corner of his eye. "Your...engineers?"

"Warrick isn't the only one here who knows his way around an engine room."

"I'm just surprised he let any of your people on board."

"Straub gave an irritated sigh. "He didn't. They spent fifteen minutes staring at the starboard fusion cannon hanging off its damn hinges and displayed their strong grasp of the obvious."

"Sure. The *obvious*."

"To be fair, you're docked at my station, taking up valuable space that could be occupied by any number of other ships that'll be coming through here in the next few weeks," Straub said.

"Is the *Solomon* due for another refit already?" Mitchell asked.

"No," she replied. "But it doesn't make for great optics having your space derelict docked here."

"Optics?" Mitchell repeated, making no effort to hide the disgust in his voice.

"People talk. We're the biggest UPA presence out here. What kind of message does it send when we've got an eighty-year-old starship parked out front that looks like it's going to fall apart if somebody looks at it funny?"

Mitchell took a breath and repeated, "Optics?"

Straub grunted. "However disgusted you are by hearing me utter the word *optics* I'm twice as disgusted."

"I don't know what you're worried about," Mitchell said as they reached the lift. "Before the end of the month we're probably going to be in the middle of an interstellar conflict between us, the Oxean and, hell, why we don't we throw in what's left of the Veneer? Once that happens, I don't think anybody is going to be too concerned about the *optics* of having my derelict space heap docked at your station."

She turned to him with a warm smile. "Well, how about that? That sounds like it'd be pretty lucky for the both of us."

Mitchell just shook his head and reached for the lift's call button. Before he touched it, the doors slid open to reveal Lieutenant Commander Marv Mallozzi standing on the other side.

"Ah. There you are," Mallozzi said upon seeing Straub.

Straub and Mitchell shared a look. "That can't possibly be good."

"I don't think Marv's ever come calling with good news," Straub said.

"For some reason you haven't been responding to your comm for the last twenty minutes," Mallozzi said.

"It's called a top-secret meeting for a reason, Marv," Straub said.

"If only the rest of the station would have the good manners to come to a standstill while you engaged in your clandestine spycraft."

She rolled her eyes "Get to it then."

Mallozzi clasped his lanky arms behind his back and took a step back as they stepped onto the lift. "You know how you're always going on about how Ambassador Reynoso is a massive pain in your ass and life would vastly improve not only for you but the sector at large if he would simply drop dead one day?"

Mitchell shot Straub a smirk.

She sighed irritably. "Yes, Marv. What specifically about these things I said to you privately do you feel necessary to bring up in the presence of my former commander?"

Mallozzi frowned. "I would hardly call the command deck in the middle of first shift 'private.'"

"Also, I seem to recall you saying pretty much the exact same thing to me not five minutes ago," Mitchell said.

"Son of a bitch," Straub muttered. "I hate you both and hope you both get Zixens diarrhea."

Mitchell scratched at the corner of his eyes, struggling to keep his grin from getting too big. "You know, as I recall, we had quite a few discussions about your temper back in the day. It's nice to see I wasn't wasting my breath."

"I learned it from you," Straub said, she twirled an impatient finger. "Get to the point, Marv. What did the fine Ambassador Reynoso do now? Vomit on another visiting dignitary? Or maybe he made a pass at the Saxon ambassador again?"

"Oh, nothing that embarrassing," Mallozzi said.

Straub breathed a sigh of relief. "Okay, well, that's a good start."

"He's simply dead."

10

"I feel I should warn you..." Doctor Randell Hogle trailed off and then gestured absently with his hand. Hogle was a spritely eighty-six-year old man with a full head of wavy gray hair. His face had a leathery, weathered look to it, and he moved with the grace and energy of a man in his thirties.

Straub folded her arms. "And?"

They sat in Hogle's office. It was almost the size of the *Defiance's* main medbay. Walls were white and had a faint shimmer on them. Hogle kept the ceiling lighting perpetually dim, but the wall shimmer made up for the difference. His desk was oversized, doubling as a conference table for when Hogle needed to speak with his staff as a group. Off to the side, on the far-left wall was a wide screen that currently had the *Atlantic's* station logo displayed on it.

Mitchell sat next to Straub, and Mallozzi stood off to the side. At this late hour it was relatively quiet in the *Atlantic's* sickbay. The only patients were a few visitors from a UPA transport ship periodically groaning in pain as they suffered through food poisoning after partaking in an Agrabon banquet.

Hogle shrugged and plucked at a piece of lint on his doctor's coat. "Well, it's really just a *feeling*. And feelings are, well, not always helpful. Warning you one way or another I don't think is going to lessen the blow. So...." He trailed off again.

Straub rubbed her forehead. "Let's just get to it. What happened? Reynoso choke on Sweezakaal stripper glitter?"

Hogle looked past her at Mallozzi. "Oh, you didn't tell her?"

Straub looked back and forth between them. "Tell me *what*?"

Mallozzi's brow furrowed in amusement. "And ruin the moment?"

"Moment?" Straub echoed.

Mitchell sat back in his chair. "Oh, this sounds like it's going to be good."

She shot him a look. "You're here as an observer. I can kick your ass out any time I want."

Mitchell nodded. "Sure thing. Consider me properly intimidated." He gestured at Hogle. "What's the punchline?"

Hogle took a deep breath. "I feel it's my duty to remind everyone here that a man is *dead*. Now, granted, he was a man who wasn't particularly well-liked by anyone in this room-"

"Or on the station as a whole," Straub interrupted.

"Dreks was rather fond of him," Mallozzi said.

Straub shot him a look.

"Well, at least he was fond of Reynoso paying his tab in a timely manner," Mallozzi said.

Hogle cleared his throat, drawing the attention back to him. "My point is, he was still a man. One would think he deserves just a tiny bit of respect."

"The absolute tiniest amount," Straub deadpanned.

"Alright." Hogle gestured towards the blank screen on the wall. "As you already know, Commodore, I spent a few years as a forensic pathologist with the Fleet's Criminal Investigations Division. I was...Well, there's no humble way of putting this: But I was very good at my job." He paused and glanced back at them. "*Very* good."

"You were supposed to be promoted to head of the division," Mallozzi said.

Hogle snapped his fingers and pointed at the Aztix with a smile. "Yes. Exactly."

Straub sighed. "Doctor, I don't have all night here."

Hogle nodded. "Of course, of course. I just wanted to establish my bona fides, if you will. I have experience in these sorts of things."

"What sort of things?" Mitchell asked.

"Well, obviously," Hogle tapped in something on his desk and the view screen on the left wall suddenly turned on, showing a live feed from the *Atlantic's* morgue. "I don't feel comfortable labeling the ambassador's death as 'accidental.'"

"Shit," Straub muttered, turning green at the sight of the body on the screen. She pressed a hand against her mouth

The body on the table looked like it had been torn apart by a wild animal. Without having been previously familiar with Reynoso it would have been impossible to determine what the body had even looked like previously. Ribs extended from the chest cavity, bent and broken at odd angles. What looked like a thick ragged cut ran from where his pelvis used to be up through the skull. Dried blood covered the corpse, along with flecks of organic material that could have only been remains of Reynoso's internal organs.

"Obviously, I was being a little cheeky before with the

whole 'forensic pathologist' bit," Hogle said. "But it's not like I was going to get another opportunity like this."

"I'm going to be sick," Straub said weakly, turning her gaze down to her lap.

"Well, yes." Hogle took a deep breath in through his nose. "That sounds about right. Like I said, I suppose I could have warned you."

"Which would have been a damn good idea," she snapped.

Hogle held up his hands, palms out for a second. "Counter-argument, though: Is there any real warning that could have prepared you for this? I don't think so."

"It would have been nice if you tried."

Hogle shrugged. "Maybe. But I prefer not to deal in 'what ifs.'"

"That looks pretty damn nasty," Mitchell said. "What the hell happened to him?"

Straub tried to look at the body again and immediately felt like she was going to vomit. She turned away sharply. "It looks like a damn Seke attack."

"It does, doesn't it?" Hogle stroked his chin thoughtfully.

Straub turned to face Mallozzi. "What the hell is this? Do we have a feral Seke running loose on the station?"

Mallozzi started to respond, but Hogle cut him off. "Most likely we don't. And if we did, we'd have heard about it long before now. But even if we did and somehow it had flown under the radar for this long, that's not what killed him."

Straub turned back to face Hogle, keeping the screen just out of her eyeline. "I beg your damn pardon?"

"That," Hogle pointed to the screen, "occurred post-mortem."

Straub pointedly did not follow his finger. She stayed focus on Hogle. "Something did...*that* to him after he died?"

Hogle nodded rather enthusiastically. "Oh, absolutely."

"Then what killed him?" Straub asked.

Hogle cleared his throat and ran a hand through his wavy hair with an air of uncertainty. "That, I'm not entirely certain of."

Straub cupped her hand over her eyes, her thumb and middle finger rubbing her temples. "Okay. Someone needs to back the hell up and start from the beginning and before any of that happens," She jabbed a finger at the body on the screen, "I need *that* off the damn screen *now*."

Hogle cleared his throat as he tapped in a new command and the screen went blank again. "I can see how that can be a distracting image."

"Sure. *Distracting*. Let's go with that," Straub muttered.

"It goes without saying, and yet I'm saying it all the same, but the body is severely contaminated," Hogle said. "From a forensic point of view. It's easy enough to determine when that damage occurred. It's harder to establish what happened before the body was disemboweled."

"Son of a bitch." Straub rubbed her hands over her face as she took a couple of deep breaths to work through the nausea. "I don't have time for this."

"I'm sure Ambassador Reynoso is finding the entire experience to be inconvenient as well," Mallozzi replied.

She shot him a look and the Aztix just shrugged.

Straub took another deep breath. "Okay. Somebody walk me through this from the top."

Mallozzi straightened up, tugging at the sleeves of his uniform. "At approximately twenty-three hundred hours we experienced a momentary power failure on V deck."

"We're having problems down there due to refurbishments," Straub said, mostly for Mitchell's benefit.

Mallozzi nodded. "My first assumption as well. However, I was then informed that this occurred twenty minutes prior to the systems reporting anything and that all of our security feeds for V deck had been wiped for the last hour prior to and including the outage. I had Commander Lin dispatch a few of her men to accompany engineering and this was what they found." He gestured in the direction of the blank screen that had previously been showcasing Reynoso's corpse.

"Son of a bitch," Straub muttered again. "And we're certain his death isn't related to the power outage?"

"Well, no." Hogle scratched at his neck. "Time of death was approximately between twenty-two thirty and twenty-three thirty, which lines up with the power outage. So, his *cause* of death could be related to the power outage. Absolutely."

Straub glared at him.

"Oh, I'm sorry," Hogle said. "Were you hoping to eliminate some options here? Even if the cause of the ambassador's death is related to the power outage, we're still looking at the possibility of somebody stumbling across the ambassador's body and disemboweling it for the fun of it."

Straub leaned back in her seat, rubbing her hands over her face. "What's Lin's take?"

"Well, considering her naturally suspicious nature, Commander Lin is operating from the basis that this is a homicide," Mallozzi said.

"Of course she is," Straub said. "Where the hell is she right now?"

"Looking for Reynoso's personal aide," Mallozzi replied.

"Thanks to the deleted security feeds, we don't know what the ambassador was doing down on V Deck."

"Nothing legal, probably," Straub said. "Are we sure we don't have any feral animals loose in the station right now? One hundred percent certain?"

"I checked the internal sensor logs myself," Mallozzi said. "There's nothing roaming our corridors that's anything less than a proper sentient being. A Bellatal freighter came through six months ago with a shipment of Seexoar cats. Despite some questionable decisions on the part of their captain and a few unruly members of his crew who had judgment impairment issues due to alcohol-related issues, none of the cats ever left the freighter. At least, they didn't leave it alive. Commander Lin turned up a handful of dealers that were selling Seexoar meat at considerable markups."

"Wonderful." Straub sat back in her chair. "Well?"

"Best guess until I can do a proper autopsy? And, mind you, I use the definition 'autopsy' very loosely in this situation. I would say..." Hogle trailed off for a moment, stroking his chin. "Some kind of violent trauma? And maybe the subsequent disembowelment was meant to cover up the method of death?"

"Lin's going to love that theory," Straub said.

"There is one more thing that I'd like to bring to your attention." Hogle reached for his desk again and then caught himself. "Actually, I think I can explain this part without the visual aid."

"Thank you," Straub said.

"Again, I haven't had a lot of time with the body and as I already mentioned, a proper autopsy is going to be a broadly defined experiment in this instance, but based on my initial examination of the body, I would go so far as to suggest that whatever disemboweled Ambassador Reynoso began as something *internal* rather than *external*."

There was a long, silent pause.

"I'm sorry?" Straub asked.

"There was something *inside* the Ambassador that wanted out and when it came out, well..." Hogle rested his hands on his chest and then pushed them out, fingers spread wide, miming an explosion.

11

"I...DON'T UNDERSTAND."

Commander Leyla Lin stared at the man sitting at the table, unconvinced. She knew Imaad Fizza as a handsome, confident, if somewhat soft-spoken man.

This was not the man sitting before her now.

This man was a nervous wreck on the verge of a complete breakdown.

The interrogation room was small. A single monitor screen on the wall to their left. A table that Fizza sat at and Lin stood over. It was just a room, really. A sparse room that to anyone else would have been mistaken for a storage room. But for Lin, it was the perfect place to hold a conversation. It didn't matter the kind of conversation. As far as she was concerned all conversation was the same: it was about discovery. Discovering something about the other person in the room. Discovering something that the other person in the room knew. Discovering something that neither of the people in the room knew to look for. All conversation was just discovery.

"What exactly are you having difficulty understanding?"

she asked him. Lin spoke with a sharp, clipped tone. Her dark hair was pulled back in a bun so tight it almost appeared as if it was pulling back the rest of her face. She was short, only a little over five feet. This didn't make her any less intimidating. "Ambassador Reynoso is dead."

"I..." Fizza faltered. He was looking at her, but his eyes weren't focused on her. It was as though his brain couldn't process her words. He swallowed and she watched as his Adam's apple bounced awkwardly. "Dead?" He blinked slowly, shaking his head. "He's...*dead*?"

Lin didn't say anything for a minute. She found that silence was often her best tool in situations like this. Let the person on the other end of the table get uncomfortable and fill the silence. They would almost always slip up and say the one thing they didn't mean to say.

Except...

That wasn't what was happening here.

Fizza dropped his head into his hands. "He's dead?" he repeated, as if he couldn't believe the words that were coming out of his mouth. As if the words were an alien language to him.

Lin folded her arms. She wasn't sure what was happening here. Everything about Fizza's behavior was coded as a man guilty of something. When she had approached him in his quarters, he had clearly been getting ready to make an attempt to leave. But this reaction didn't square with that behavior.

What the hell was going on here?

She leaned forward, pressing her hands against the table. "Imaad." She almost snapped his name, trying to get his attention focused back on her. It worked. He looked up at her, his expression startled, almost surprised that she was in the room with him. "What's going on here?"

His eyes dilated for a second. Something flashed there. She tried to identify it: Fear? Suspicion? Relief? What the hell was it? Whatever it was, it was gone with a blink of his eyes.

Fizza shook his head. "I don't know."

"You don't know?" she echoed. "That's an interesting take." Lin took a breath, biding her time. "We found Ambassador Reynoso on V Deck. Do you know anything about that?"

Fizza flinched. The mention of V Deck definitely triggered something.

"Why was he down there?"

"I..." He dropped his gaze from her. "I don't know."

"You don't know?"

"I think I'm in shock," he said, his voice sounded hollow.

"Shock," she repeated.

"This is..." Fizza swallowed and placed both of his hands palms down on the table. "You just told me my boss is dead."

"You didn't like your boss."

His gaze flicked back up to her. "What?"

"This isn't a shock," Lin said. "Nobody liked him."

"I don't understand."

"He was a degenerate alcoholic. He had ongoing relationships with several known prostitutes and it was believed he owed a healthy sum to three different loan sharks in this system. Also, he had a bad habit of vomiting on visiting dignitaries."

Fizza rubbed his temples. "He thought that a sip of Backlon brandy would help steady him before conducting a meeting. It never did. Instead, it simply upset his stomach. I tried to explain this to him every time and he never listened."

"Was that an ongoing problem?"

"What?"

"His difficulty listening to you."

He paused; brow furrowed. "What is this?"

Lin didn't answer him.

"How did Ambassador Reynoso die?" Fizza asked. His voice was growing steady. His body language was calming down.

What the hell was she missing?

The frantic expression in his eyes was replaced with genuine confusion.

"That's what I would like to know," Lin said.

"I don't understand."

Lin gestured to the screen.

Fizza turned in time to see an image of Reynoso's corpse appear.

He audibly gasped as the color drained from his face. His left hand, still on the table, was pressed tightly against the surface in what appeared to be an attempt to keep himself from falling out of his chair. "*What...?*"

The image disappeared from the screen.

Fizza's gaze dropped from the screen to the ground. He took several deep breaths, trying to steady his nerves. He glanced up briefly at the screen again, almost hesitantly so, as if afraid the image would reappear. When it didn't, he half-turned back to Lin.

"What the hell was that?" he whispered.

"That was Ambassador Reynoso," she replied. "Or, at least, what's left of him."

Fizza's mouth flapped open and closed for a few seconds. He gently shook his head, as if trying to clear a mental image that wouldn't go away. His fingers pinched the bridge of his nose as he squeezed his eyes shut. "What happened?"

"Like I said, that's what I'm trying to figure out."

He looked at her, not saying anything. There was something playing out across his face, something he was clearly struggling with. He licked his dry lips and said, "Am...am I under investigation?" Lin shrugged. He added, in a quieter tone, "Am I...a *suspect*?"

"Suspect," Lin repeated, like she was trying the word out for the first time. "Suspect. That's an interesting word choice."

"I don't understand."

She held out her hand. "Well, from my point of view you seem to be behaving in a very suspect manner."

Fizza twitched, his gaze momentarily flicking away from her.

"But that," Lin nodded at the blank screen. "I don't know what that is. We don't know what killed him. Could be an accident."

"An accident?" He latched onto the word like a thirsty man desperately grabbing a bottle of water.

She shrugged. "Could be something else."

Fizza took a breath, clearly trying to steady himself. "Then why am I here?"

"Why are you here?" she repeated. "Because, presumably, you were one of the last people to see him alive."

"That...that sounds like an accusation."

Lin nodded, but didn't say anything.

"I didn't kill him," Fizza said, sounding far more confident with those four words than anything else he had said.

"Okay. You didn't kill him." Lin took a step back, pressing her hands down the sides of her uniform, smoothing it out.

"You don't believe me."

Lin just shrugged, again not saying anything.

Fizza swallowed nervously and struggled to maintain eye contact with her. "I'm not lying."

She shook her head gently. "Oh, you're definitely lying about something."

He twitched again.

"A dead ambassador isn't something that's just going to quietly go away."

"I don't think he's going to be making a lot of noise now," Fizza said, his voice straining slightly.

Lin didn't crack a smile. While she was generally considered to be an excellent investigator, she had never been able to discover a sense of humor.

"Jokes aren't going to help your case," she said.

Fizza's gaze hardened. "I didn't kill him."

Lin pursed her lips together. Again, she didn't say anything for a moment.

"I didn't kill him," he repeated. "I didn't even..."

"Okay," Lin said abruptly, softening her tone and pulling back from him. "When was the last time you saw the ambassador?"

Fizza blinked, momentarily startled by the sudden shift in her tone. "I...what?"

"When was the last time you saw Ambassador Reynoso?"

Fizza licked his lips, blinking rapidly before finally breaking eye contact with her. "I, um, I don't remember."

"You don't remember?" She repeated, unconvinced.

He wiped at his forehead. "It was early this evening. I don't remember specifically when."

"So, you do remember?"

"It's been a busy night."

"Oh? What have you been up to this evening? Planning a trip?"

Fizza twitched nervously again. "If I'm not being investigated-"

"You still may have some vital information."

"I don't know anything," he said, his voice almost a whisper.

"I don't believe that."

"I think I should have my lawyer present."

"You could," Lin agreed. "I'm certainly not going to stop you."

Fizza glanced at the door, but he didn't move.

After a moment, Lin asked, "What was Ambassador Reynoso doing down on V Deck?"

Fizza was suddenly focused on his fingernails.

"I don't know what you're trying to hide from me," Lin started.

He looked up at her sharply. "I'm not trying to hide anything."

She pointed at him. "That's another lie."

Fizza opened his mouth as if to argue with her, but quickly thought better of it.

"At some point, I'm going to find out what he was doing on V Deck," Lin continued. "There's enough people on the station, somebody'll spill something eventually and it won't take a lot of work. Because, like I already reminded you, nobody liked Ambassador Reynoso. As soon as his death is made public, I'm going to have a line of people standing outside my office eagerly waiting to tell me some scandalous detail they heard about the ambassador."

"Then what am I doing here?" Fizza asked.

The question was asked a little too boldly in Lin's opinion.

"You're here because I don't want to have to waste time separating fact from fiction," Lin said. "A dead ambassador sets off all sorts of alarms in Fleet Admiralty. It's not good, even if it's an accident." She paused. "So, you want to tell me what he was doing down on V Deck?"

Fizza studied the surface of the table for a minute. He rubbed the tips of his fingers against the table as he struggled with some kind of internal debate. Finally, he gave a deep sigh and met Lin's eyes again.

"Ambassador Reynoso was on V Deck to meet with Viv'an Bendare."

12

"WHAT THE HELL is *Viv'an Bendare* doing back on *my station*?" Straub was furious, practically shouting across the room at Lin.

Lin held up both hands apologetically. "As far as I know, nothing. Because she's not on board."

Straub jabbed a figure at her. "Are you *sure* about that?"

"I personally escorted her off the station myself," Lin said. "I tagged all of her passports, known pseudonyms, aliases and connections. There's no way Bendare can be back on the station without me knowing about it."

Straub redirected her finger to the screen behind Lin with Fizza on it. "He seems to think she's here."

Lin folded her arms. "Well, I'm inclined to think he's lying."

"You think everybody's lying."

"Usually with good reason," Lin said.

Straub dropped her arm and then let the rest of her body drop into the seat across from Lin's desk, groaning. "Shit. I don't like the way this is going."

Lin leaned back against the edge of her desk. Her office

was sparse to the point of being nearly empty. There was no personal touch to the room and the only indication that it was routinely used by anyone was an immaculately cared for Bonsai tree on her desk. "What does Hogle have?" Lin asked.

"A biohazard mess," Straub said, rubbing her temples. "At this point, he's still not ready to rule out some kind of viral infection."

Lin frowned. "I can't recall a viral infection that leaves a body in that condition."

"I can't either, but Hogle rattled off six of them and two were Phulkin based," Straub said. "And if it's a viral infection, then we've got a much bigger problem than just a dead ambassador."

"Fizza should know if the ambassador was exposed to anything."

"That sounds like a good question to ask him," Straub agreed, making a vague gesture indicating that Lin should go back into the room and do just that.

"Except I think there's something else going on here," Lin said.

"Because you think he's lying."

"Of course he's lying. Look at him." Fizza sat there, fidgeting awkwardly. His disposition had improved, but only marginally. He still seemed very much on the edge of a breakdown. "He's too damn nervous."

"Yeah, well, I'd be nervous too if my boss just turned up dead and I was sitting on news that Viv'an Bendare was on the station." Straub took a breath. "What did he say?"

"Specifically?" Lin sat down behind her desk. "Not a damn thing. I had to pull every little bit out of him, word by word."

"Then it should be very specific."

Lin rolled her eyes. "Earlier this evening he received a private message over one of the encrypted dark servers. He didn't think anything of it because, after all, Reynoso was a degenerate scumbag who spent a lot of time dealing with people who liked to communicate over encrypted dark servers."

"I really can't believe this is actually happening," Straub muttered, cupping her hands around her face. "Sure, I didn't think the guy was going to live a long life, but I had hoped that when he did die, he'd be in somebody else's jurisdiction. Or, at the very least, he'd have the decency to die like the degenerate he was: Choking to death on a peanut while having sex with a Sweezakaal prostitute. Embarrassing for him, but not exactly a mountain of paperwork for me. This? Whatever the hell *this* ends up being? Too much damn paperwork for this asshole." She shook her head.

"Paperwork?" Lin echoed.

"We all don't have wet dreams about filling out paperwork."

Lin made a sour face. "I find it *relaxing*."

Straub twirled an impatient finger. "What did this alleged message say?"

"Bendare had some information for Reynoso."

"What kind of information?" Straub asked.

Lin didn't answer right away.

"What?"

"I haven't seen the message myself," Lin said. "I've got somebody downloading everything from Reynoso's private accounts right now."

"That's a hell of an overstep if this turns out to be an accident," Straub said.

"I figured it was better to ask for forgiveness instead of permission," Lin replied.

Straub smirked. "Okay, so?"

"You're not going to like it."

"As if there's going to any part of all this I do like."

"Well, at the end of the day, Reynoso's no longer a headache for you."

"Which is only a good thing if he doesn't become a bigger headache in death. What was Bendare's message?"

Lin took a deep breath before answering. "Blackmail."

"Shit," Straub muttered. "Whose?" But she already knew the answer.

"Reynoso's," Lin said. "Apparently he's been in contact with the Veneer Empire."

13

ZEMBLE FOUND himself back in Calloway's room.

He wasn't sure why he was back there. He just couldn't figure out any other place to go.

He had wandered the *Atlantic* aimlessly for a few hours, thinking that maybe he might stumble across...something? Another church? A familiar face from Pastor Loring's church? Maybe even Pastor Loring himself? But it was late and the only people he came across looked even more lost than him.

Cavige hadn't lied. A quick search of the station's news logs had turned up an article on Loring's problems and subsequent departure. The article didn't contain any details on why no one had bothered to step up and lead the church in Loring's absence.

Zemble didn't like it. It felt *wrong*. It felt...

There was that tingle in his horns. That tingle that told him there was something off about the whole situation. But there wasn't much he could do about it now. Loring had to be halfway back to Earth and no one on the station seemed all that broken up about it.

So Zemble found himself back on the *Defiance* and then, soon after that, back at Calloway's side.

He eased his large frame back into the chair he had been occupying earlier and leaned forward, his chin resting on his folded hands and his elbows propping him up on the backs of his legs. He sat there and watched as Calloway's chest rose and fell with each breath.

The problem was, Zemble knew what the problem was. He wanted to pretend that he didn't know. He wanted to be one of those people who couldn't see all the clues before them and just stumbled through life blissfully unaware. But that wasn't who he was.

So, he knew what the problem was.

Yes, it was partly what he had told Sadler. But there was another part to it. After all, there was a reason he was here in Calloway's room and not his own quarters.

Zemble felt lost.

Emotionally.

Spiritually.

And physically.

Nothing he had called home felt like home anymore. The time he had spent wherever Steve had sent him had... Well, it hadn't changed him. But maybe it had changed his perceptions? Or perhaps even more simply, because after all, Zemble was a man who wasn't very good at bullshitting himself, but maybe he had spent so much time in that other place, it felt more like home than his own home did.

Zemble grunted incredulously at this thought.

He recognized his quarters. He knew his way around the ship. He remembered all his shipmates and friends. But it all seemed distant, like he was visiting a location he hadn't been to since he was a child.

Time had no meaning over *there*. At least not in any way

he could understand. A second could have been an hour. A year could have been a second. But Zemble knew he been there for some time. A long period of time, in fact.

Except only seconds had passed here, on the ship, in his home.

Seconds.

Years.

Moments.

Decades.

How was he supposed to reconcile that in his mind?

Why should he have to reconcile that?

Why wasn't he just lying on a bed next to Calloway in a catatonic state? It would certainly make more sense than whatever state he was in now.

Zemble grunted again.

Nothing felt right anymore.

Food didn't taste right. His bed didn't feel right. His interactions weren't right. Maybe no one else noticed something was different with him. Most likely no one else noticed. But he noticed. He *knew*.

And again, he knew what was missing. He didn't want to know. He wanted to be blissfully ignorant. He wanted to drift through the rest of his life with this vague sense of something being not quite right, but never being able to pin it down exactly.

But that wasn't him.

So, he knew.

It was the pain.

Zemble missed the *pain*.

That *place* Steve sent him...Everything *hurt*. Even when they weren't doing anything to him, everything *hurt*. It hurt so bad. He would spend hours screaming from the pain.

Endless pain.

Never-ending pain.

Pain.

Pain.

Pain.

That was the first thing he noticed when he came back. The pain was gone. One second it was there, consuming him, and then it was simply gone.

More than anything, he knew that was the problem.

Nothing felt like home.

Nothing felt *right*.

Zemble closed his eyes.

God help him, he *missed* the pain.

And he didn't know what to do about it.

He knew he should be grateful the pain was gone. He knew that he should be happy he was home and pain free.

Except this place didn't feel like home without the pain.

Zemble wanted to pray about it. His first instinct was to open up his heart and pour out his soul to God about it.

But almost immediately, he stopped himself.

He wasn't certain what he was praying for. What he was praying *about*.

Was he thankful to God that the pain was gone?

Or was he angry that God took the pain away?

And what the hell was wrong with him if it was the latter?

So, trapped in a state of indecision, Zemble couldn't pray.

He had been ceaseless in his prayers in the other place. They were, he knew, the only thing that kept him sane during those seconds, those decades.

But here, back home, back in this familiar place...

Nothing felt right anymore.

Zemble opened his eyes again, half expecting Calloway

to be sitting up, looking at him. But no, she still laid there, unmoving.

And Zemble was no closer to an answer.

He rubbed his eyes.

"Forgive me, Father," Zemble said quietly and said nothing else. Because he didn't know what to say. He didn't even know what he was asking forgiveness for.

So, in absence of anything else, he picked up the datapad he had left on the small table next to Calloway's bed and powered it on. He cleared his throat and began reading again from the book of Genesis.

14

Keane woke up confused.

First, he couldn't remember where he was. It was dark and the bed he was in was unfamiliar. It was less...lumpy than he was used to.

He felt naked, literally in this case. He lifted the sheets that were crumpled across him and confirmed that, yes, he was definitely naked.

So, he was naked in an unfamiliar bed.

A soft groan alerted him to the body in the bed next to him.

He glanced over, his eyes finally adjusting to the dark, saw the naked back of a dark-haired woman in the bed next to him.

So, he was naked in an unfamiliar bed with a woman. Things were looking better. But none of that explained the part that he was confused about.

Keane got up, swinging his legs over the edge of the bed, careful not to disturb the sleeping woman. He couldn't remember her name. But in his defense, he was pretty sure she hadn't offered a name last night at Dreks'.

What he did know was that she was an ensign in the *Atlantic's* astrometrics department and she responded all too well to his line about how she was too pretty to be working in astrometrics. It was a terrible line and he immediately regretted using it. But she really was very attractive. She was exactly his type: short, athletic, pouty lips and immediately into him. But still, he should have been better than, "You're too pretty to be locked up in astrometrics all day." But Ensign Pouty Lips didn't know that, and she ate it up, hook, line and sinker. Keane sighed. It didn't hurt that she had already been about six shots of Vulderran vodka into her night, so it was possible that her judgment had already been slightly impaired. And...

Keane paused; his uniform halfway zipped up. Actually, that was the problem.

She had been drunk.

Keane had consumed easily twice the amount of booze last night. Probably more. And then, of course, there was the Proog Doldoss' Blitz Delight.

And here he was, wide awake with nary a hangover in sight.

Keane glanced at the time on the nightstand. It was half past oh-six-hundred hours. What the hell was even doing up at this hour? He, Warrick and Nax had gotten started at nearly midnight and by the time he had met Ensign Pouty Lips, it was nearly three in the morning. And now it was three hours later and he was wide awake and very much not hungover.

He zipped up the rest of his uniform and turned in a half circle, trying to remember where her bathroom was. His first guess landed him in an even darker closet. Behind door number two he found what he was looking for.

With the door closed securely behind him, he turned the lights to full and took stock of himself in the mirror.

The face staring back at him was the same face that had been staring back at him for the last thirty-five years. He didn't look particularly old, but then he didn't look particularly young either. His jet-black hair was still free of any gray strands and the wrinkles that had plagued his father at this age hadn't set in yet. He ran a hand over his scruffy beard and once again thought about shaving it all off. But without the beard, his babyface was apparent. People had a hard time taking him seriously as a commanding officer when he looked like a fresh-faced ensign right out of the Academy. When he hit his fifties, he'd probably be happy about that, but until then he needed to manufacture some way to make sure people respected him.

Keane took a deep breath.

Ensign Pouty Lips had to have been at least ten years his junior. It was the only logical explanation. Only a twenty-five-year-old would fall for a line about being too pretty to work in astrometrics. A twenty-five-year-old who didn't know how to handle her booze.

He frowned. Why was he being so hard on himself about this? He was known to be perfectly charming in various circles. There's no reason why she couldn't have found him just as charismatic without the added help of Vulderran booze. In fact, the Vulderran booze probably dulled the impact of his natural charisma.

The thought of the Vulderran vodka brought him back to his confusion: Where the hell was his hangover?

Sure, for a brief moment he had been confused when he woke up. But that was just normal, waking-up-in-a-bed-that-wasn't-his-own confusion. It happened to him every time he went on shore leave and within a night or two, he was fine. Unless, of course, he made a new friend and ended up in a different hotel room.

Keane shook his head, trying to clear out the unnecessary clutter in an attempt to stay focused on the central question that was bothering him.

Last night he had wanted to test the limits of his newly restored body. Thanks to the accident at Serenity Base, it had previously taken an unusual amount of exotic alcohol to achieve any kind of basic buzz for him. His body simply didn't process alcohol the same as it did before he had to have forty-seven percent of his internal organs replaced.

But now, according to Marlize, he might as well be factory fresh. The computer said he was completely, one hundred percent organic. Not a single piece of plastic, metal, or anything artificially fabricated anywhere in his body. Not only that, but the computer even said he was a good ten years younger than he really was. And now that he really stared at himself...

Keane leaned forward, propping his hands on the sink. There was no telltale sign of any exhaustion on his face. No bags under his eyes. No facial twitches. No droopy eyelids.

There was no way he had a restful night's sleep. Not after all the drinking he did with Nax and Warrick and especially not after what he and Ensign Pouty Lips did once they came back to her quarters.

He didn't seem to be suffering any of the traditional memory loss that came with excessive drinking. He didn't feel dehydrated, sick, or woozy. In fact, he felt...Great?

Keane took a step back from the mirror, frowning.

Great?

Nobody feels great after a night like last night.

Hell, last he had seen of Warrick before heading off with Ensign Pouty Lips he was so wasted he was getting ready to start dancing on a Daboo table in the middle of Dreks. It was going to make a hilarious story to tell later and Keane almost didn't want to miss it. But that was around the time Ensign Pouty Lips had grabbed at his crotch and whispered in his ear about how she had spent six months on Nanan learning Sweezakaal gymnastics.

So.

There was no way Warrick was even up right now. It was physically impossible.

Keane dug around in his pockets, looking for his communicator. He came up empty and remembered that the *Atlantic* had a weird communication feature built into most of their private bathrooms.

He tapped the corner of the mirror and a digital overlay appeared over his reflection. He punched in the *Defiance's* prefix, followed by Warrick's personal number. After a few seconds, somebody on the other end answer.

"Warrick?" Keane asked.

The person on the other end uttered a Vulderran curse that was so vile and profane that it actually caused two different civil wars on Vulder Prime and had been illegal to even speak out loud during the last one hundred years. The person alternated between whispering and shouting the curse a few more times and then immediately broke the connection.

"Yep. Definitely Warrick," Keane muttered to himself.

Definitely Warrick and Warrick was definitely in no condition to communicate right now.

Keane tapped the corner of the screen again and the digital overlay disappeared. It was just him and his reflection again. So what the hell was he doing here right now?

A soft chime from the bedroom pulled his attention away from his current state. He opened the bathroom door, hoping to slip back out and grab his communicator before it woke Ensign Pouty Lips. He was too late.

She had propped herself up on one elbow, looking around the room, confused, her eyes squinting shut against the light coming from the bathroom. "What?"

"Sorry," Keane said, picking up his communicator from the nightstand. "That's me."

She blinked, staring at him, clearly struggling to remember who he was. The sheets fell from the top part of her body and Keane was immediately reminded about the other part of her that he had been attracted to.

Something clicked in her head and recognition dawned in her eyes. "What's going on?" she asked, rubbing her tired eyes. She glanced at the time on her nightstand. "Why are you even up?"

"That is a very good question," Keane said. "And I wish I had an answer for you." He glanced at the name on his communicator. It was Captain Mitchell. "I'm gonna have to take this."

She patted the empty spot on the bed that he had been occupying a few minutes ago. "Come back to bed." She dropped back against her pillow. "I'm gonna make you my famous buttermilk pancakes." Her eyes were already shut again and the last few words out of her mouth were less of a coherent sentence and more of a tired slur.

Before Keane could even give a half-hearted excuse, she was already back asleep.

His communicator beeped at him again.

He paused before answering, gazing longingly at Ensign Pouty Lips's inviting form.

The communicator beeped, as though it was taking personal offense at Keane for not answering.

He sighed and answered as he ducked out into the main corridor. "Go for Keane."

"Good morning, Commander," Mitchell said.

"It's starting to feel like one," Keane agreed.

"I heard you had quite the night out last night," Mitchell said.

"You did?" Keane paused. "What, um, exactly did you hear?"

There was a pause long enough from Mitchell's end that Keane started to get uncomfortable. "Enough to wonder if you were going to be conscious enough to answer my call."

"Well, to be fair, sir," Keane said. "We are docked for repairs. It's not exactly like I had a lot on my to-do list."

Mitchell didn't respond to that and Keane could practically hear the disapproving frown coming from the other end.

Keane cleared his throat. "But, ah, you probably don't want to hear my justification for getting wasted while technically on call."

"Some things are best left unspoken."

"Yes, sir. I totally agree. To answer your question: Yes, I am available for duty."

"Mr. Warrick isn't," Mitchell said.

"Apparently Warrick can't handle his booze as well as I can," Keane replied.

"Hopefully we won't need any emergency repairs to the ship before he sobers up."

"As I understand it, based on the stories I've heard, Hungover Warrick is basically an engineering wizard," Keane said.

"I'd rather not find out."

"Neither would I," Keane admitted. "I am not currently

on the *Defiance*, but I should be back within twenty minutes."

"Don't bother."

"I'm sorry?"

"Report to Commodore Straub's office. I'll meet you there."

"I'm confused, what's happened on the *Defiance*?"

"Nothing," Mitchell said.

"Now I'm really confused."

"There's been a death on the *Atlantic*. I'm having the case transferred to you."

"Commander Lin is a fine investigator," Keane said. "I'm sure whatever this is, she's more than equipped to handle it."

"That may be," Mitchell agreed. "However, she's missing one vital thing for this particular investigation."

Keane paused, feeling awkward in the empty corridor. "Is it...a penis?"

"*What*?"

Keane shook his head. "I don't know why I asked that. Please forget the words even came out of my mouth."

"It's *security clearance*," Mitchell said, sounding a little short. "Commander Lin lacks the security clearance to handle all the details of this case."

"Right. Of course. That makes a lot more sense. Wait, what is this? Who's even dead?"

"Ambassador Caldwell Reynoso died last night," Mitchell said. "And it's connected to the Veneer."

15

"LIEUTENANT, correct me if I'm wrong, but I'm pretty sure you've got yourself a fairly comfortable private suite on this ship. You don't even have to deal with the indignities of having a roommate."

Zemble got up from the chair he had fallen asleep in. It creaked in relief as he lifted his considerable bulk from it. On the bed, Calloway lay there as unresponsive as she had been the night before. He made a half-hearted effort to smooth out the wrinkles in his uniform and then decided that he really didn't care. Doctor Rabkin had already found him asleep in Calloway's room.

"Sorry," Zemble said, trying to make his way through the doorway. But Rabkin didn't move.

"No need to apologize," Rabkin said with a dismissive wave. "I don't have any rules about friends of my patients crashing overnight. Besides, I'm sure she enjoyed the company."

Zemble glanced at the readings on the screen above Calloway's bed. Everything was still the same as it had been before: No significant brain activity.

"I don't think she noticed I was here," Zemble replied.

Rabkin shrugged. "Who can say what she noticed and what she didn't."

Zemble looked at him, surprised. "Aren't you supposed to know?"

"Well." Rabkin stroked his chin. "I can tell you what the science says. I can tell you what my computers say. Hell, I can tell you what my gut says. But I'm not exactly a psychic. I can't just jump into Ms. Calloway's head and tell you, definitively, what she may or may not be experiencing."

"That's remarkably openminded of you," Zemble said.

Rabkin shrugged. "I like to hedge my bets. Also keeps me from having an overwhelming God Complex. Point is, I don't mind you being here, I don't think she minds you being here, but I'd be lying if I didn't say I wasn't a little damn curious as to how you fell asleep here in the first place."

Zemble's face was deadpan. "Just lost track of the time."

Rabkin raised his bushy eyebrows. "Lost track of the time, eh?"

"That's what I said," Zemble replied evenly.

Rabkin held up both hands. "I'm not looking to start a fight."

Zemble's face crumbled into a frustrated frown. "A lot of people have been saying that to me lately."

Rabkin's bushy eyebrows went up again. "Oh? Is that so? And why do you suppose that is?"

Zemble didn't answer right away, not entirely certain if Rabkin was expecting an actual answer. When he realized that Rabkin had no intention of moving from the doorway, he sighed and said, "Clearly people seem to be mistaking my behavior as more aggressive than I intend it to be."

"Is that so?" Rabkin stepped into the room, making his

way around Zemble without really so much as a look. He stood over Calloway, holding her wrist in his hand to personally check her pulse as he examined her vitals on the screen. "Any speculation as to why that keeps happening?"

Zemble paused before answering. He stared at the open doorway for a long moment and then with a sigh that Rabkin almost didn't notice, he turned around and replied, "Has somebody spoken to you recently?"

Rabkin shook his head, gently lowering Calloway's wrist back down. He leaned over her, brushing a few strands of hair off her forehead and then placed two fingers on the other side of her neck, just under her jawline. "I don't need anybody to speak to me when I find you losing track of the time in one of my patient's rooms."

Zemble grunted. "Fair enough."

"Well, it's that strong handle on the obvious that's made me the doctor I am today."

"Personally, I think it's the horns."

Rabkin glanced up at the horns extending from Zemble's forehead and smirked. "The horns?"

"People find them unsettling."

"Makes you look aggressive when you're just a big ole teddy bear?"

"That's my current theory."

"You feel comfortable with that theory?"

"As comfortable as I'm going to feel with any theory," Zemble said.

Rabkin straightened up, double-checking the information on the screen. He frowned.

"What's the matter?" Zemble asked.

"Other than the fact that she's in a coma and I can't explain why?" Rabkin asked, looking over his shoulder at him. "Well, I'm a little worried about you."

Zemble blinked, momentarily taken aback. "I'm sorry?"

"It's obviously not the horns, Lieutenant."

Zemble shrugged. "Well, I'm a security expert, not a doctor."

"And I'm a medical doctor, not a psychological one. But something tells me you wouldn't go talk to a psychiatrist if I recommended one."

Zemble pointed at Calloway. "It didn't help her."

Rabkin took a breath and then exhaled slowly. "Well, sure. That's because her problem was she was infected with another alien entity." He pointed to Zemble. "You're clearly suffering some kind of post-traumatic stress disorder."

"That's what your diagnosis of Calloway was as well."

Rabkin frowned again. "And I'll be the first to admit that I was wrong. But in my defense, it's not like I had all the facts."

"What makes you think this situation is any different?"

Rabkin didn't answer right away. His bushy eyebrows bunched up as he studied Zemble. "Maybe it is. You bring back any symbiotic hitchhikers that our scans missed?"

"Not that I'm aware of."

"Then until something suggests otherwise, I'm going to cross it off the list of possibilities."

Zemble grunted reluctantly. "Fair enough."

Rabkin held out his hands, palms out. "Then there you go. We're in agreement. You're not possessed by a previously unknown alien entity that's causing your behavior to seem slightly more aggressive than usual."

"I'm definitely going to sleep better tonight," Zemble said.

"Maybe even in your own quarters?" Rabkin suggested.

"Maybe," Zemble agreed. His communicator chirped

with a message. "I need to report to the *Atlantic* for a security meeting."

"I know you're still a little reluctant to go back to your quarters. But." Rabkin pointed to his rumpled uniform. "You might want to change first. People will take you more seriously if you look less like a damn space hobo."

16

"IT SHOULD GO WITHOUT SAYING, but as of this moment, this entire case is classified Top Secret." Mitchell paused, looking around the room, as if waiting for a contradictory response.

"And yet, you said it," Zemble grumbled.

Mitchell looked at him. "Are you having a problem, Lieutenant?"

"Not at all, sir," Zemble said.

Keane frowned, looking over at his second-in-command. "You look like shit."

Zemble gave him a sideways glance, but didn't say anything. Keane just shrugged.

"Anybody else have any more nonsense they'd like to add to the proceedings?" Mitchell asked, eyeing them each individually.

Keane straightened up in his seat, tugging at the collar of his uniform. "No, sir."

Zemble replied with a wordless, deadpan look.

"Right." Mitchell gestured to Straub. "It's your show."

"Oh, joy of joys," Straub grumbled, getting to her feet. She looked very much like a woman who hadn't gotten any sleep the night before. Keane wished he knew what his secret was, because it sure looked like she could use whatever he was on.

The conference room was small, to the point of almost being claustrophobic. This had more to do with the room's lighting and less to do with its actual size. In reality, the room was large enough to comfortably fit a dozen or so people. The lighting, however, created corners covered in shadows that shortened the room. And then coupled with Zemble's presence, everything looked even smaller.

Officially, this conference room did not exist. Along with a handful of other sections on the *Atlantic*, it had been removed from the official documentation of the station. The internal sensors did not acknowledge its existence. It contained no recording devices. It was, essentially, a black hole in the middle of the *Atlantic* that nobody happened to notice.

Straub pressed her hands against the table and took a deep breath. "Most of what I'm about to say is intended to bring the two of you up to speed, as your captain and I have been dealing with this for the last twelve hours. So if either of you gentlemen happen to know any of this, please feel free to stop me so we can move this along." She exhaled and gestured to the screen behind her. A picture of Reynoso appeared on the screen. It looked like it had been pulled from his security clearance file. In the photo he was clearly ten years younger and far less prone to late night alcoholic binges. "Twelve hours ago, Ambassador Caldwell Reynoso was found dead." She paused, waiting to see if either of the security officers would cut her off.

"Well, I did know about this," Keane said. "Of course, I only just found out about it thirty minutes ago when Captain Mitchell contacted me about it."

Straub glared at him.

"That's probably more of the nonsense you weren't interested in."

She cleared her throat. "Here's something you didn't know: This was the condition he was found in on V Deck shortly after a power outage."

The image behind her switched to one of Reynoso's disemboweled corpse.

"Well, shit," Keane said, shifting uncomfortably in his seat. He looked away, holding up a hand to the side of his face and peering through the slits of his fingers at the screen. "You could have warned us about that."

Straub nodded. "Yes, I certainly could have. But nobody warned me and I'm a big believer in passing along the pain. Also, you were being an asshole."

Zemble just grunted, apparently unfazed and gave the image on the screen his full attention.

Keane looked at him sideways. "Seriously?"

"I've seen worse," Zemble said.

"When?" Keane asked.

"Well, for starters, when they brought you back from that ghost ship and half your body had been torn off you."

Keane opened his mouth and then closed it, uncertain how to respond to that. Instead he turned his attention back to Straub and tried to not stare at the image on the screen, which was difficult given that Straub positioned herself directly in front of it.

"Whatever did this is not what killed him," Straub continued.

That triggered Keane's curiosity more than the image trigged his nausea. He dropped his hand and leaned forward. "I'm sorry, what?"

"Doctor Hogle has determined this..." She gestured absently with her hand back at the image on the screen. "Whatever you want to call it, occurred post-mortem."

"Interesting," Zemble said.

"Sure. *Interesting*," Keane replied. "That's a word we could use to describe this."

"In addition to the power outage, all the security feeds from V Deck were erased," Straub continued. "Everything from at least thirty minutes prior to the outage and thirty minutes after the outage is gone. As of right now, the only witness we have confirming that Reynoso was headed down to V Deck is his personal aide, Imaad Fizza. He's even given a reason for the ambassador going down there: He was supposed to meet with a contact that was allegedly black-mailing him."

The screen behind Straub changed again. This time a purple skinned woman with jet black hair and a voluptuous figure appeared.

"This is Viv'an Bendare."

Keane pointed at the screen. "Okay, now *her*, I know about."

"About damn time," Straub said, rubbing her forehead. "I was afraid I was going to have to walk through this whole damn thing step-by-step."

"Who is she?" Zemble asked.

Straub glared at him.

Zemble just folded his arms and didn't say anything.

Keane cleared his throat. "I got this one." He nodded at the profile on the screen. "Viv'an Bendare is one of the richest citizens in the UPA. She's worth nearly six billion credits."

"Sounds like she's a pretty shrewd businesswoman," Zemble said.

"Well, her primary business is as a black-market arms dealer."

Zemble's face didn't change. "Still, tough market to get into these days. Especially with the Oxean Syndicate expanding their reach."

"She inherited most of her business from her father," Keane said. "A Chirotian businessman who ran one of the largest illegal gun running operations in the Siter Sector. About six years ago he ended up dead and Bendare ended up with the entire operation dropped in her lap."

"Sounds like she expanded quite a bit," Zemble said, glancing at the information on the screen. "The operation her father was running would have been small change compared to what she built it into."

"Well, sure," Keane said. "But, hey, why does it feel like you're trying to defend this lady?"

Zemble shrugged. "Mostly just to screw with you."

Straub folded her arms. "I'm sorry, Lieutenant, are we keeping you from something?"

"Best guess," Keane said. "I'd say we were keeping him from doing his laundry. I don't think I've ever seen an officer in a uniform this unkempt."

Zemble growled at the back of his throat. "My apologies, Commodore. I had a difficult night."

"Really? More difficult than finding out an ambassador died under extremely suspicious circumstances while on your watch?"

Zemble fidgeted in his seat. "I just had an uncomfortable night's sleep."

She nodded. "Well, I didn't get any sleep."

"Sorry," he said.

"I don't want your apologies, Lieutenant. I want you to get your act together."

"I assure you, ma'am, the current state of my uniform notwithstanding, my act is completely together," Zemble said. "Full disclosure: Some of my behavior is simply the result of my desire to give Commander Keane a hard time."

Straub rubbed the side of her face. "Are you serious?"

"It's the nature of our relationship."

She looked at Keane.

"He's not wrong," Keane replied. "We enjoy being assholes to each other."

Straub looked at Mitchell. "You want to jump in here?"

"I said it was your show," Mitchell said.

"Yeah, it might be my circus, but these are your monkeys," she replied.

"She also diversified beyond just black-market arms," Zemble said, twisting in his seat to get a better view at this screen. "A small prostitution ring out of the Siter and Voiliv Sectors, illegal loan services, and, what looks like a very extensive blackmail network. These aren't easy markets to break into, especially when you're trying to crossover like she did."

"Okay, now you're just trying to see if you can get me in trouble," Keane said.

"Not completely," Zemble said. "But it is rather impressive that she managed to turn her father's small arms business into an intergalactic crime consortium."

"Are you being serious here?"

Zemble nodded. "A little. Anybody else around here think she killed her old man to take over the family business? Seems like a pretty obvious move to me."

"She launders all of her profits through a real estate business," Keane added. "Moves over a billion credits in land parcels through the Aurrod and Qeebvav systems alone. It's one of the primary reasons she hasn't been charged with anything yet." He scratched his beard. "Although, I remember reading a security report about how you got her kicked off the station, though, using some old decency law loophole."

Straub inhaled through her nose as she pressed her hands together, fighting the urge to yell at everybody in the room. "Yes, technically we trespassed her."

Zemble raised an eyebrow. "You trespassed her?"

Straub exhaled slowly. "Obviously I couldn't get her arrested. She has some of the best lawyers in the UPA and better people than I have tried to get her implicated in *something*. What I could do, however, was exercise a little-known section of Article Fifty-Seven in the Treaty of Nimoy, which allows station commanders to ban individuals from UPA property indefinitely. However, there's no specific wording on reasons for why you might ban an individual, because when the treaty was drafted everybody was high on the notion that the United Planetary Alliance wasn't going to have any apples so bad they would actually need to be kicked out. In my case, Bendare, in general, behaved herself while onboard the *Atlantic*, alleged illegal activities notwithstanding. But fortunately for me, she likes to walk around basically half-naked all the time." Straub grinned. "So I had her kicked off on the grounds of being indecent. So now, she's not allowed anywhere within a mile of the *Atlantic*. Which, since we're a starbase in the middle of nowhere, means she can't come back on board. Honestly? It's a messy solution. I don't particularly like it. But it got her out of my hair, and that still counted as a win in my book."

"This is who Reynoso was going to meet?" Keane asked.

"According to his aide, yes."

"Doesn't really seem like somebody who runs in his social circles," Keane said.

"And yet, they had a long history together before I had her kicked off the station," Straub said. "Maybe what they say is true. Opposites really do attract."

Zemble raised an eyebrow. "They were romantically connected?"

Straub nearly burst into laughter. "No, but Bendare has a history of having helped Reynoso find..." She made a disgusted face. "We'll call it *romance*. But in this particular instance, her contact with him was less about helping him and more about blackmailing him."

"Over what?" Keane asked. "I can't imagine Reynoso would be bothered if it came out he was using prostitutes. Hell, half the station knew about it, didn't they?"

Behind her the screen changed again, this time to a screenshot of a text message Reynoso had received shortly before his death.

"So here's the kicker, the reason why this is getting kicked over to you fine gentlemen. And no, it's not about Reynoso's need to pay for sex. According to Bendare's message, Reynoso has been in regular contact with a ranking officer in the Veneer Empire."

"Okay," Keane said. "That's interesting, but not exactly worth blackmailing. After all, he is supposed to be the UPA's representative to the Veneer."

"One might even say that he was actually doing his job," Zemble said. "Not something most people get blackmailed over."

"Except that Reynoso hadn't logged any of these contacts," Straub said. "They'd been going on for the better part of six months. As far as the diplomatic corps was concerned, we still hadn't heard from anybody in the Veneer Empire for over a hundred years."

"Still." Keane rubbed the back of his head. "I know about blackmail. And nobody gets blackmailed because they weren't documenting a historic conversation."

"What about setting up a drug trafficking network, Commander?" Straub asked, her tone getting sharper. "Does that meet your criteria for blackmail?"

Keane held up a hand. "I want it on the record that I'm not here to start a fight."

"Why the hell would Reynoso be interested in getting into the drug trafficking business?" Zemble asked.

"Because the drug in question is kameko," Straub said and the screen behind her changed again. An image of a red crystal appeared on the screen.

"Well, shit," Keane breathed, leaning back in his chair. He glanced at Mitchell who just shook his head with a grim expression.

"In case either one of you has forgotten," Straub continued. "Kameko is the most potent hallucinogenic known to date. It can be artificially created through very extensive means. These means are also very expensive, so thankfully it's not exactly something that's flooding the UPA right now. It does, however, occur naturally on three planets: Volla, the residents of which are currently in the middle of a civil war and are liable to blow up anybody who goes poking around their planet looking for illegal drugs to harvest. Then we have Monov. Here kameko is routinely destroyed. The Monovean government has a task force whose sole responsibility is to find fields of kameko and burn them to the ground. As such, it's obviously not something that's available in very large quantities. And finally, there's Niunus

Two-Three-Five, a small moon deep in Veneer space that is home to the largest naturally occurring quantities of kameko known to date. Of course, it's Veneer space and the only people in there these days other than the Veneer are the Oxeans and, for whatever reason, they've never been interested in kameko. But they sure as hell don't mind blowing up anybody who happens to be headed that way."

Straub straightened up and took a step back from the table. She pressed her hands against her cheeks before running them through her graying hair.

"According to what we've pieced together from Bendare's messages, Reynoso believed it was possible, with the help of his new Veneer contact, to set up a supply chain running from Niunus Two-Three-Five to a small Alvi colony in the Neutral Zone and from there, distribute kameko at nearly thirty times its traditional value, thanks to its rarity."

Nobody said anything for a few minutes. Each one of them took the information and let it stew in their minds as they poured over the details piece by piece.

Finally, Zemble said, "This is unbelievable."

"Yeah," Keane said. "No kidding. Our first contact with the Veneer Empire in almost a hundred years and it's our own ambassador setting up a new illegal drug trade route. Somehow I don't think this is the kind of diplomatic break-through we were hoping for."

"No." Zemble leaned forward, folding his hands on the table. "I mean that this is *literally* unbelievable." He pointed to the screen behind Straub. "Everything that I know about Ambassador Reynoso suggests he's an alcoholic degenerate with a severe gambling problem who hasn't been sober in years. It's impossible to believe he cooked up this plan."

Keane pointed at Zemble. "That is actually a very good point."

"Yeah," Straub said. "You're not the only person who's thought of that. But the messages were clearly directed to Reynoso, inviting him down to V Deck, where we did find his dead body. Like I said, suspicious circumstances."

"Where's his aide?" Zemble asked. "This Fizza character?"

"Still onboard the station," Straub replied. "You're also not the first person who's thought of that. Commander Lin brought Fizza in to question him about the ambassador's whereabouts and Fizza was, well, shifty as hell. The man looked like he had just committed murder himself."

"Are we sure he didn't?" Zemble asked.

"Security logs show him going from the ambassador's office to his personal quarters and staying there until Commander Lin picked him up," Straub said. "In addition, we don't know what killed Reynoso, so we don't know what we should be looking for anyway. But he seems awfully guilty about something. We've frozen his passport as well as his accounts. He won't be going anywhere for at least twenty-four hours."

Keane raised a finger. "That seems like a remarkably specific number all of a sudden."

"That's because it is the exact amount of time we have before my station report, which includes the death of Ambassador Reynoso, gets filed on the network and ends up on the desks of the admiralty back on Earth and, subsequently, the office of President D'Ambra. Once they have this news, things are going to get a lot worse for a lot of people."

"The only thing worse than an ambassador setting up an illegal drug trade route would be our political system doing it," Mitchell said.

Keane blinked, looking back and forth between them. "That's not a thing. There's no way that's a thing."

"That is most definitely a thing," Mitchell said. "The D'Ambra Administration wants into the Veneer Empire. They would jump all over this the minute it fell into their laps."

"Who's going to tell them?" Keane asked. "I'm sure as hell not going to." He turned to Zemble. "Are you?"

"I wouldn't even know who to tell," Zemble replied flatly.

Keane turned back to Straub. "And, hey, while we're at it, why don't we just delete the messages? That seems like it would solve a lot of problems."

"Except that it wouldn't. For starters, as Reynoso's personal data is protected under Article Twelve of the UPA's Constitution and is considered classified information, such an act would be illegal. Hell, the fact that Lin pulled it in the first place, is a real gray area right now. But, also, if it's true, Bendare is still out there with the information that brought Reynoso down to V Deck in the first place."

Keane took a deep breath and exhaled slowly. "I don't like this."

"Good. You can join the club. Admission is free. But we're thinking about adding annual dues."

Keane laced his fingers together and rested them on the table. "Commander Lin's already been working this case for the last twelve hours now. How much momentum is going to be lost by kicking it over to us?"

"Probably more than I would like," Straub said. "But it's not my call to make. Once the Veneer connection was uncovered, Admiral Wanamaker wanted to keep this within the purview of Directive Fifty-Two and Commander Lin doesn't have clearance for that. And despite your ship's casual relationship with security clearance, I could not convince Wanamaker to loop in Commander Lin." She clapped her hands sharply. "So, here we are. Any more stupid questions about why this is getting yanked from the hands of my capable officers and dumped in your laps?"

"Nope," Keane said quietly as he shifted uncomfortably in his seat. "That pretty much covers it."

"Good. So here's what I want from you two fine gentlemen: I want to know what happened to Reynoso. There's no way his death was an accident and it seems unlikely that it wasn't related to this cockamamie kameko scheme," Straub said. "In addition, I want to know what's actually going on with this damn thing and how to kill it before anybody in the UPA finds out about it."

"And what about Bendare?" Keane asked.

Straub snapped her fingers and gave them a sour grin "Yes. That's right. *Her*. I want to know where the hell she is and how the hell she got back on my station. Because, apparently, she shouldn't be here without us knowing and yet, she seems to be here and I didn't know about it. I really don't like that."

"I imagine you wouldn't," Zemble said.

She shot him a look. "Do I really look like I'm in the mood for your nonsense right now, Lieutenant?"

"No, ma'am," Zemble replied with a deadpan expression.

"Most of all, I want you to handle all this like the consummate professionals you're supposed to be." She paused and held up a finger. "No, I take that back. I want you to handle this like the professional that *Commander Lin* is. Because she would handle this without setting off any damn alarms or starting any fights on my station. And that's how I expect you to handle this. Any questions?"

Zemble and Keane looked at each other and then back at Straub.

"No, ma'am," Keane said.

"Good," she snapped and stormed out of the room.

Keane turned to Mitchell and opened his mouth.

Mitchell shook his head, cutting him off. "I wouldn't, Commander. I really wouldn't."

17

"WHAT DO YOU THINK?" Keane asked, tugging at the collar of his uniform.

"I think about a lot of things," Zemble replied as they rode the lift up to E Deck. "My mind is constantly occupied with observations of the world around us, so you're going to have to be more specific."

"You really are working on being an asshole today, aren't you?"

"I know," Zemble said. "I should be in a better mood. It's not every day we get a murder investigation dropped in our lap. I'll try to remind myself to be more grateful."

Keane rolled his eyes. "What do you think about the case?"

Zemble grunted and folded his arms. "I think this Fizza character is damn suspicious."

"Yeah, that stood out to me, too."

"Clearly he's been in communication with this Veneer contact under the guise of Ambassador Reynoso," Zemble continued.

"It makes more sense than Reynoso actually doing it," Keane said.

"Reynoso was a wreck of a human being," Zemble continued. "Fizza was probably running the entire office. He was controlling all of the information in and out. Hell, he was probably handling all of the official communications as well. Think about it, what's more likely: Reynoso sobering up long enough to file any kind of regular reports or Fizza handling all of the paperwork? It could be why Reynoso's been out here as long as he has. Fizza's been covering his ass."

"And he wasn't doing it out of the kindness of his heart if he was setting this thing up on the side."

"Given Reynoso's condition, the nature of our current relationships with the Veneer, he was probably counting on the fact that nobody was ever going to suspect anything."

Keane slipped two fingers under his collar on either side of his neck and yanked at it like he was trying to stretch it out. "So why'd he kill Reynoso?"

Zemble didn't answer right away.

"Tripped up your theory there?" Keane asked.

"Not exactly," Zemble said after a moment. "Fizza probably didn't kill him."

"Excuse me?"

"It would work against him to kill Reynoso as evidenced by the fact that here we are suspecting him in trying to traffick a highly illegal hallucinogenic out of the Veneer system."

"Something killed Reynoso."

"Obviously," Zemble agreed.

"And then something did whatever that was we saw done to him."

"That was probably something he ate," Zemble said.

Keane looked at him. "Seriously?"

"Orand beans have been known to cause internal combustion if not properly prepared."

"They're also not allowed on any UPA vessel for that very reason," Keane said.

"Obviously it wasn't orand beans," Zemble replied. "I was simply using that as an example." He watched as Keane yanked on the front and back of his collar at the same time. "What's the matter?"

"Doesn't fit right," Keane replied.

"Seems to be a problem for you lately," Zemble said.

Keane stopped yanking at his collar and looked at Zemble. "What's that supposed to mean?"

Zemble clasped his hands behind his back. "It means I've noticed that you've been having some difficulty feeling comfortable in your uniform since your miraculous recovery."

Keane looked him over. "At least I don't look like a damn space hobo."

Zemble made a noise at the back of his throat, but didn't say anything.

"What's the matter?" Keane asked.

"Nothing."

"Hey, seriously. I was out drinking all night. I should be the one looking like he slept in his uniform. What the hell were you up to?"

"Keeping Calloway company."

Keane raised both of his eyebrows, but didn't say anything.

Zemble rolled his eyes. "I was reading the Bible to her last night and I fell asleep in her room."

Keane opened his mouth and then closed it. After a

second he said, "Somehow that's worse than what I was thinking."

The lift jolted to a stop as it reached E Deck and they stepped off.

"How is that possibly worse?" Zemble asked.

"I don't know. It's weird."

"Weird?"

"Do I have to spell it out for you?"

"It would be helpful in this particular instance," Zemble said.

Keane shook his head. "It's weird and you know it's weird."

"Also took some time to pray for her."

"That makes it weirder."

"I like to think it's helping her."

"Praying to your imaginary old man who exists in some alternate dimension just out of our reach, sitting around listening to us whine about our pitiful existence and occasionally granting wishes? You think that's going to help her?"

"You mess it up on purpose at this point, don't you?"

Keane shrugged.

"I'd like to remind you that you were practically dead and then miraculously revived and restored," Zemble said.

"So you're saying that your God is an alien from a higher dimension who also goes by the name Sharon?"

"No, I'm saying that you shouldn't be so quick to brush off a miracle," Zemble said.

"I don't think you reading bedtime stories to a comatose woman is going to result in a miracle."

"No," Zemble agreed. "But praying for her might."

"If you say so."

"It's not me who says so," Zemble said. "It's written in the Bible."

"The one that you're reading her?"

"Yes."

Keane threw up his hands. "I honestly don't know what I'm supposed to say to any of this. How am I supposed to take you seriously when you talk like this?"

"Is that a serious question? Because I have a few suggestions," Zemble said.

Keane shook his head.

"There is something I've been meaning to ask you," Zemble said after a few minutes.

"About what?"

"Did you see anything?"

Keane glanced at him, confused. "What? When?"

"When you were almost dead. Before Sharon restored you. Did you see anything?"

"What do you mean?" Keane asked as they rounded the corner.

"It's a fairly straightforward question," Zemble said.

"The hell it is."

"You were practically dead," Zemble pointed out.

"That's still a long way from being actually dead," Keane said.

"It's a shorter distance from where you are now."

Keane shot him a look out of the corner of his eye. "What the hell is that supposed to mean?"

"Same thing as it meant before," Zemble said. "You were nearly dead. In fact, I believe it even qualifies as a near-death experience."

"I'm not talking about this with you."

"It seems only reasonable to discuss what you may or may not have seen," Zemble continued.

"And that's why I'm not discussing this with you," Keane said.

Zemble nodded. "My father had a near-death experience when he was a little younger than I am. He claimed to have seen a bright light."

"It was probably from the operating table."

"In the light, he saw what he believed was an angel."

Keane sighed irritably. "Zemble..."

"You were nearly dead," he repeated.

"I didn't see anything."

"All due respect," Zemble said. "I doubt that."

"You *doubt* that?"

"At the very least you should have experienced some kind of hallucinogenic reaction to the Unity invading your body."

Keane came to an abrupt stop. He twisted in the corridor and tried to bring Zemble to a stop as well. But thanks to his size the only way Zemble was going to stop was because he wanted to. Keane's hand caught him briefly on his chest and then Zemble pushed passed him before stopping a few steps away.

Keane put his hands on his hips, glaring at him. "You're really working hard today on the asshole thing."

Zemble just shrugged.

"What's your endgame here? What exactly do you hope to accomplish by hounding me about all this?" Keane asked.

"I wouldn't say that I'm hounding," Zemble said.

"That's because you're not on the receiving end."

"But my idealized ending of this has you turning your life over to Jesus Christ and becoming a born-again believer."

Keane stared at him, unblinking. "I literally have no idea if you're joking right now."

"I'm not."

"You say that, but it doesn't help."

Zemble shrugged. "I concede that I probably should use a defter touch in talking to you about this. But is there a more naturalistic way to bring up the redemption of your immortal soul than by talking about your near-death experience?"

Keane shook his head and resumed walking. "I should have you transferred to another ship."

"Is that supposed to be a threat?" Zemble asked, following after him. "Because our ship is a floating death-trap. Every night I pray to be delivered from it. It's how I start my nightly prayers."

"Of course it is," Keane muttered.

"So having me transferred would actually work in my favor. First, I get on a ship that isn't threatening to fall apart every time we jump to lightspeed. Second, and this is the more important part, you get to see the power of prayer. That can be a transformative thing to experience."

"You are my least favorite person right now."

"I can live with that," Zemble said. "Jesus wasn't popular with the nonbelievers either."

Keane came to a stop and double checked the name on the door. "Here we are." He tapped the call button on the wall next to the door. "Be a professional and try not to open up our interrogation with a moment of prayer."

"I prayed silently while we were on the lift," Zemble said. "So you don't have to worry about that."

Keane glanced back over his shoulder at Zemble's deadpan expression. "I would really like to be able to tell if you're joking."

"I would really like it if people stopped assuming I was trying to start a fight with them," Zemble said.

Keane opened his mouth and then closed it when he realized he had no idea what to say. He turned back to the door and hit the call button again. When another minute went by without Fizza answering, Keane said, "Screw this," and punched in a security override.

A second later the door slid open. On the other side the apartment was dark.

"Mr. Fizza?" Keane announced loudly.

There was no response.

They stepped into the apartment as Zemble said, "Computer, lights to full."

Keane blinked for a second against the sudden burst of light.

"Aw, shit," he muttered.

Dangling from the ceiling, a thick piece of rope wrapped around his neck, was Imaad Fizza's lifeless body.

18

"Brace yourselves, gentlemen, because I'm really going to knock your socks off with this one: Yes, his injuries are consistent with a man who committed suicide," Hogle said.

Zemble grunted, clearly unamused.

Hogle then added with significantly less theatrics, "More or less."

"More or less?" Keane echoed.

The three men stood over Fizza's body on the exam table. A digital hologram hovered a foot above Fizza's corpse. It was a detailed reconstruction of his entire body.

Hogle chewed on a strawberry flavored protein bar as he gestured at the hologram, focusing on Fizza's collarbone. "There are several broken bones here. It's to be expected in a person who hanged themselves. However, this," he pointed to the hyoid bone, located just above the Adam's apple, "is what we might call an unusual break in this situation."

Keane leaned forward for a better look, but nothing about the break seemed unusual to him.

Hogle watched him and said, "Mind you, such a break can occur in hangings, and has, especially among older victims. That being said, this particular break is more common in victims of strangulation."

Zemble and Keane shared a look.

A handful of crumbs dropped from Hogle's mouth and onto Fizza's cold chest. He brushed them off absently.

"And in case either one of you were wondering, Mr. Fizza just celebrated his twenty-eighth birthday earlier this year. So I don't think anybody here would classify him as an 'older' victim. Of course," Hogle continued. "It may simply be that at the last second Mr. Fizza had second thoughts about ending his life prematurely and struggled just enough to break this particular bone." He shrugged. "Or maybe it's nothing at all."

"How long has he been dead?" Zemble asked.

"Oh, excellent question, Lieutenant. Let's see." Hogle double checked the data. "Time of death was an hour and a half ago. Give or take a few minutes."

"Ninety minutes ago," Keane said. "Shit."

Zemble held up his datapad. "I've got reports of him being seen on the main promenade this morning. But he skipped out on two appointments he was scheduled for."

"Who were the appointments?"

"Ambassador Taushav and the second one was just marked as personal," Zemble said. "This is the work calendar he shared with Reynoso."

"We need to get access to his private one."

"Already on it."

Hogle finished off his protein bar. He brushed the crumbs from his hands. "How 'bout that? Both Fizza and Reynoso dead within less than twenty-four hours of each other. That's a hell of a thing, isn't it? Might even say it's a suspicious thing."

"You got something specific you want to share?" Keane asked.

Hogle raised a finger. "As a matter of fact, I do." He took them over to a screen on the opposite side of the room and Reynoso's body appeared. "As I'm sure the commodore has already explained to you, I've spent the last twelve hours trying to put Reynoso's body back together in an attempt to find a cause of death."

The disemboweled corpse slowly faded into a digital representation that was slowly pieced back together to resemble Reynoso prior to being disemboweled.

"So, first off, and I don't know what you know about the ambassador, but his blood alcohol level was significantly high. Which is very normal for him. However, what wasn't normal, was while it was high, I'd seen it much higher," Hogle said.

"So he wasn't that drunk?" Keane asked. "Weird detail to latch onto."

Hogle made a face and dipped his hand side-to-side. "With Reynoso, you had to adjust a lot of what your normal expectations were. Pick any other human, yourself for example. If you came into my office with a blood alcohol content level that was even half of what Reynoso's was, I'd have your stomach immediately pumped and put you on a strict detoxing program in hopes that I could keep you alive a little bit longer. Reynoso, however, had a much higher level of resistance. This was not something he was necessarily born with. But rather he built it up through years of careful practice. He was one of the strongest drunks on the Atlantic."

Zemble grunted. Keane glanced over his shoulder at him, but Zemble pointedly kept his focus on the datapad in his hand.

"I honestly can't remember the last time when he had been even remotely sober," Hogle continued.

"Please tell me this has a point," Keane said. "Because I don't think his prowess as an alcoholic is going to factor into this."

Hogle wagged a finger at him. "I wouldn't be too sure about that." He tapped the screen and an image of a beetle-shape creature appeared. "I'm guessing you don't know what a baalhanno beetle is."

Keane shook his head.

"I didn't think you would. It's a relatively obscure parasite from the third moon of Donis," Hogle said. "The percentage of individuals who contract this parasite are... Well, it's a lot less than even one percent. Mostly due to the fact that the third moon of Donis is, apparently, an absolute nightmare to visit. But there are a few brave souls who do venture down there and occasionally, they get infected. Now, for the most part, they'll go the rest of their lives without knowing they've even been infected. The baalhanno is a relatively benign parasite. It feeds mostly on fatty cells and the average person, human, Elwat, or otherwise, has plenty of those to go around. The baalhanno isn't particularly greedy, so it's not as if it's feeding on huge chunks of fat. You don't suddenly discover you've dropped three pant sizes overnight."

Keane folded his arms. "Please tell me this is going somewhere, Doc. Because right now it just feels like you're using this opportunity to impress me with your knowledge of obscure parasites."

Hogle paused and then asked with a small smile, "Are you impressed?"

"No, not really."

Hogle winked. "Don't worry, we're getting to the punchline. See, Reynoso had one of these parasites. We're not entirely certain who he contracted it from, but knowing him, it was probably from a prostitute. That's not saying anything against sex workers. They just happen to be the only people who have gotten close enough to Reynoso to pass anything along like this in years."

"He sounds like he was an absolute charmer of a person," Keane said.

Hogle shrugged. "He had his moments. They were few and far between. But he had his moments." He rubbed his hands together. "So, here's the fascinating thing about baal-hanno: They feed on fatty cells and can be quite content on them. But they get absolutely *addicted* to alcohol." He smiled. "Starting to see how this might be relevant? The baalhanno have a reaction not unlike an addict's. They need constant alcohol to maintain any semblance of normalcy. And when they don't get it, the host pays the price, usually through some kind of sickness. Often it presents itself as a stomach ache with flu-like symptoms and the baalhanno will die off if the host abstains for any length of time. For whatever reason, the baalhanno can't go back to surviving on the fatty cells. Something in its genetic makeup has changed permanently with the introduction of alcohol.

"This, of course, was never a problem for Reynoso. Because, as I already mentioned, the ambassador kept a blood alcohol level that would kill anyone else. So the baal-hanno in his system? They were well fed.

"Except for last night." Hogle gestured at the screen. "Not only was Reynoso's blood alcohol level much lower than normal, but it also looks like there was an increased amount of synthehol in his system. Synthehol is, of course, a synthetic variant of alcohol that contains no intoxicating or addictive properties. It's popular among the people who want to look cool because they're drinking, but don't want to be bothered with any of the side effects of drinking alcohol. Synthehol has plenty of side effects of its own, not the least of which is liver damage that can be up to fifteen percent more damaging than just drinking regular alcohol. Generally speaking, I try to discourage my patients from drinking it. I personally don't think it's a good idea to be pumping your body full with that much artificially created garbage on a regular basis. Reynoso wasn't a fan of it either, yet here it is in his system in massive quantities.

"So, since for whatever reason, Reynoso was having his fill of synthehol, the baalhanno in his body were starved for proper alcohol. They went after the next best thing, unable to tell the difference between the real stuff and the fake stuff. Which brings us to a question that nobody ever thought they would ask: What happens when baalhanno parasites feed on synthehol? Well, now we know the answer."

The screen switched back to Reynoso's corpse.

Keane made a face. "Is that what killed him?"

Hogle shrugged. "Probably? I don't know for certain. But what I do know is that it sure as hell didn't help his overall condition." He paused for a moment, rubbing the tips of his fingers together as he studied the image of Reynoso's corpse. Finally he turned back to face Keane. "Personally, and mind you this is pure speculation on my part, but I believe that with the amount of synthehol he had in his system, I think there might have been somebody else out there who knew this was going to happen."

"That's a hell of a leap to make," Keane said.

"Sure. But I wouldn't be much of a doctor if I couldn't make that kind of leap."

"You're going to have to draw me a line connecting those dots."

"Any other physician would look at the synthehol in Reynoso's system and brush it off. Or, worse, ignore it completely," Hogle said. "Being that I've been treating the man for a variety of conditions and ills for the last eight years, I have a different perspective. I see the synthehol there and I see something that's not supposed to be there at all." He held out his hands. "It's the very definition of 'suspicious.'"

Keane rubbed his chin, forcing himself to look at Reynoso's corpse again. His stomach churned a little. He wasn't a man that was easily sickened by things. But this was...*grotesque*. Possibly one of the worst things he had ever seen. And to think it had been caused by a parasite...

"Hell of a way to kill a guy," Keane said.

Hogle shoved his hands into the pockets of his lab coat. "It sure is."

"Assuming it was done on purpose, you'd have to know about Reynoso's condition," Keane said.

"Yes, it certainly narrows down a potential pool of suspects."

"Who else knew about the parasites?"

Hogle took a deep breath. "Well, there was me and a few of my medical staff. But that's all I can say for certain. I wasn't privy to who Reynoso would have shared the information with."

"But they're easily transmittable? So didn't he have to tell...people?" Keane asked.

Hogle nodded. "You're thinking of his liaisons with prostitutes." He coughed into his hand. "Well, for starters, no. Reynoso probably wouldn't have told any of them. He wasn't the type to be concerned with other people's wellbeing. Secondly, and this is the more relevant part, the treatment plan he was on kept them from being transmitted to anyone else. Short of donating blood, and I can assure you one hundred percent there was no way in Hell that was ever going to happen while I was the CMO here, it just wasn't possible for him to infect anyone else."

"What are the odds Fizza knew?"

"Very good," Hogle replied. "Fizza handled a lot of the ambassador's personal affairs as well as his professional. In fact, Reynoso had cleared him to view all of his medical records. I routinely passed off test results to Fizza to be disseminated to Reynoso when the ambassador was unable to make it in for an appointment."

"And now Fizza's dead."

"By suicide, no less," Hogle said. He bunched up his shoulders and his eyes got a little wide with excitement. "Makes you wonder all sorts of things."

"Yeah, it sure does." Keane looked back at Zemble, but the large Elwat wasn't even paying any attention. His focus was on the datapad. "Hey, you catching any of this?"

"No," Zemble replied curtly.

Keane sighed. "What the hell?"

Zemble looked up at him and turned the datapad around. "I got access to Fizza's personal calendar. I know where he was supposed to be this morning: the Church of Eternal Clarity."

19

"MADAM COMMODORE-!"

Straub cut off the tall, green haired Bethari with a sharp wave of her hand. "I really don't have time for this right now, Ambassador Taushav."

Straub made a move to walk past the heavyset Bethari, but the ambassador moved at a speed that an individual with her body shouldn't have been able to.

"You will *make* time, Commodore." Ch'Koran Taushav was tall for her species, but still shorter than most humans. She was almost as wide as she was tall. Her skin was dark black with violet veins close to the surface. Like all Bethari, her hair consisted of a dozen or so six-inch thick strains that were a shade of green that often seemed to glow. She had narrow, shallow eyes that took up most of her face and a nose that seemed to fold directly into her mouth. She was considered one of the most difficult ambassadors on the station to deal with. Taushav believed that every problem could be solved with a hammer, regardless of whether it needed something more delicate.

Straub looked down at her, trying to decide if it was

worth the trouble of actually calling security and having her removed from her office.

"Ambassador, I've had a difficult morning. The last thing I want to add to my to-do list is getting into a pissing contest with you," Straub replied.

Taushav scowled at Straub's vulgarity. "I had an important...*meeting* with Ambassador Reynoso scheduled for this morning."

Straub nearly rolled her eyes. Half the station knew what kind of 'meetings' Taushav and Reynoso engaged in and they were hardly the stuff of political intrigue. Taushav indulged in many of the same terrible habits and behaviors that Reynoso had. The difference between the two ambassadors was that Taushav still knew how to sober up and do her damn job in the morning.

Taushav locked her eyes onto Straub's to drive home the next four words. "He never showed up."

Straub moved her hands behind her back as she struggled to keep a neutral expression. "That sounds like something you should really take up with Ambassador Reynoso's office." She gestured to the doorway behind Taushav as a way of suggesting it was something the ambassador should go do right now.

Taushav failed to take the hint. "As a matter of fact, I *did*."

Straub pressed her lips together to keep herself from shouting a few choice obscenities at the ambassador. Instead she simply said, "Then I'm not quite sure what you're doing *here*."

Taushav's face darkened. "Commodore Straub, I am not interested in playing games here."

"Neither am I," Straub replied. "So, if you'll excuse me, I have a station to run."

Again, Straub tried to move past her and, again Taushav didn't budge.

Taushav placed her thick, fleshy fists on her hips. "I will *not* excuse you, Commodore. Not until I get some *answers*."

"I can't give you answers to questions you haven't asked," Straub replied curtly.

"No one seems to be at Ambassador Reynoso's office."

"That's still not a question," Straub said, her tone growing terser with every passing second. "If your concern is regarding Ambassador Reynoso's office hours, then I strongly encourage you to bring that up with his office."

Taushav twitched her head and her thick strands of green hair flopped over her shoulders. "Very well, Commodore, then I will *ask* you a *question*."

Straub held out her hands expectantly. "That sounds wonderful. I cannot wait to hear this all-important question."

Taushav folded her arms. "Where is Ambassador Reynoso?"

Straub didn't hesitant. "I have no idea."

Taushav glared at her. "That is not an acceptable answer."

"Then it's a damn good thing I'm not answerable to you," Straub said, leaning into the irritation she felt, regardless of whether or not it was valid. "Ambassador, I run a station that has, at any given moment, fifteen thousand individuals on board, seven thousand of those are permanent residents. I have neither the time nor the ability to keep tabs on all of these people."

"Very well, Commander, I'm going to cut to the chase."

Straub threw her hands up. "What the hell have you been doing so far?"

"I've heard some disturbing rumors regarding Ambassador Reynoso."

"If they're about how he paraded his naked ass in front of the female delegation from Gundor, it's all true," Straub replied. "But I would imagine you knew that already."

"The rumors I've heard suggest that he's *dead*."

Again, Straub didn't hesitate. "That seems to be a hell of a leap to make just because he's not answering your calls."

Taushav didn't say anything for a moment. Instead she focused intently on Straub's face, as if she could divine the unspoken truth.

"If this is going to devolve into a staring contest, then I concede right away," Straub said. "Especially if it'll make you go away."

"He's been missing since at least this morning," Taushav continued. "And more than one person has suggested to me that something happened to him last night."

"More than one person?" Straub asked.

"I have my sources, Commodore," Taushav replied, a touch defensively.

"Good for you," Straub said. "But I can't say that I'm exactly thrilled to have a network of people spreading unfounded gossip on my station."

"Is it unfounded?"

"That's what I just said."

Taushav pulled back her thick lips, baring the tips of her upper teeth. "If something's happened to Reynoso you are *obligated* to tell me."

"Obligated?" Straub echoed, ignoring the intended Bethari power play Taushav was making with her teeth. It was the sort of move female Bethari made to establish dominance. It had fallen out of practice over the last century or so. But many Bethari in various political positions over the last decade had slowly been bringing it back in an attempt to court a younger demographic that felt as though the individuals in power were simply toothless puppets of the UPA. "You have a strange interpretation of what *my* obligations are," Straub said.

"A man is dead-"

"According to rumors," Straub said, cutting her off. "What else did these rumors tell you? Maybe they mentioned how he allegedly died? Or *where*? Hell, if you give me a location right now, I'll have Commander Lin send a few of her men down to check it out."

Taushav made a disgusted clicking noise with her tongue against the back of her teeth. "I don't appreciate this game you are playing."

"So, that's a no, then?" Straub sighed. "That's genuinely too bad. I really thought there was something useful that was going to come out of this whole conversation."

"Reynoso and I are engaged in multiple affairs," Taushav said. "Both business and personal."

Straub raised a bemused eyebrow, but didn't say anything.

"It's not unreasonable to assume that if something has happened to him," Taushav continued, "there is a possibility that something could happen to *me*."

"All due respect, but that sounds like you're greatly over-valuing yourself," Straub said.

Taushav scowled again and jabbed her thick, fleshy finger at Straub. "If something's happened to Reynoso it is eventually going to be made public. You cannot simply hide it forever."

Straub placed her open palm against the length of Taushav's outstretched finger and gently pushed it down. "You would be amazed at the full scope of my abilities,

Ambassador," she said. "I know that I sure as hell am. Trust me, Ambassador, I am certain that if something had happened to Ambassador Reynoso, you would be the very first person we would contact."

"I don't like your attitude."

"Well, fortunately, I don't need your approval to survive," Straub said.

Taushav shook her hand at Straub, the fleshy rolls along her forearm flapping like dirty laundry. "I *will* find out what's happened to Reynoso."

"That sounds great. If you discover anything interesting, can you please let me know?" Straub asked. "Because before all this, I didn't really give a rat's ass. Now though? You've really piqued my curiosity. I'm going to need some closure on this one."

Taushav scowled and spat off something in her native tongue before storming out of Straub's office.

Straub sighed and dropped herself in the chair behind her desk.

Taushav wasn't wrong. Eventually the station was going to find out that Reynoso, and now his damn aide, were dead. And it was probably going to slip out a lot sooner than twenty-four hours if Taushav was already hearing rumors.

Rumors.

Who the hell was spreading rumors in the first place?

It had to have been one of Hogle's nurses. They were a gossipy bunch. She was going to have to have a talk with him. Not that it was going to help if the news was already spreading.

"Commodore?"

Straub looked up, slightly startled at the sound of a new voice, half afraid it was Taushav back for another round. Instead she found Commander Lin standing in her doorway. She gestured to the seat across from her desk. "Leyla, what can I do for you?"

Lin stepped into the office, but didn't sit down. She stood behind the chair; her hands clasped behind her back. "Is there a reason I'm not heading up this investigation?"

Straub frowned. "Yes, because I said so."

Lin made a distasteful expression. "I don't find that answer to be satisfactory."

"No, I imagine you wouldn't," Straub agreed. "But it is what it is."

"I'm not fond of that saying either."

"Yeah, neither am I," Straub agreed. "Unfortunately I'm finding that more often than not it's the only thing I can say when there's nothing else for me to say that isn't going to get me in trouble."

Lin raised an inquisitive eyebrow.

Straub shifted in her seat. "I don't know if you've heard, Leyla, but I apparently have a reputation for making grown-ass adults weep like little babies."

"I've heard of one or two incidents," she replied.

"I'm trying not to do that anymore," Staub said. "Apparently it sets a bad tone for station morale."

"Have people just considered not being whiny babies?" Lin asked.

Straub sighed. "You know, if anyone else said that I'd think they were making a joke." She nodded at Lin. "What can I do for you, Commander?"

"Permission to speak freely?"

Straub didn't answer right away.

"Ma'am?" Lin prompted.

Straub held up a finger. "Gimme a second. I'm thinking about it."

"You're...thinking about it?"

"Nothing ever good follows that request. Especially with you."

Lin tightly pressed her lips together, irritated.

"Last time you asked me if you could speak freely you ended up shouting at me," Straub said. "Now, while I didn't burst into tears, it wasn't exactly something I cared for."

Lin grimaced. "I promise you I won't be shouting this time."

"Right. Sure." Straub sighed and twirled a finger. "Permission granted. But let's remember, I'm still allowed a lot of leeway in how to discipline my subordinates. Last time I hesitated in having you tossed out an airlock. I don't think I'll hesitate this time."

Lin looked her directly in the eyes. "You shouldn't have taken this investigation away from me."

Straub sat back, folding her hands across the desk. "Okay."

Lin continued, "As you've already pointed out, you're allowed a certain amount of leeway. And, yes, I understand you were joking about tossing me out an airlock. But the fact remains, out here, *you* are the boss. Out here, the *Atlantic* tends to exist as its own entity. Technically, we may be representatives of the UPA. However, we are lightyears away from any real help, assistance or influence from the UPA. In fact, it would take months for the UPA Admiralty to even make their way out here. Out here, we are as alone and independent as any other member of the UPA. In fact, we function much like a planetary member of the Alliance. We certainly have the crime statistics of one. Planetary members of the UPA don't expect that their problems will be swept up and handled by outside resources. They understand that they're responsible for their people, their problems, their messes. That's the *Atlantic*. This death

occurred on our watch, our soil, and we should be responsible for it."

"I don't disagree with you," Straub said.

Lin opened her mouth and then didn't say anything. A
puzzled look spread across her face.

"You weren't expecting that response, were you?" Straub
asked.

"It comes as a bit of a surprise," she admitted.

Straub got up. "You're not wrong, Leyla. I agree with
everything you just said."

"Then, if you'll excuse me for saying, but what the hell?"

"There's a chain of command."

"I'm familiar with the concept," Lin said.

"Good. I'm glad," Straub replied dryly. "The people
above me don't agree with you. Guess who overruled my
call?"

"I think that maybe I wasn't clear," Lin said.

"No, you were very clear. I understood you perfectly,"
Straub said.

She pointed to Straub. "You're out here on your own."

"Heading up a starbase with a population of nearly
fifteen thousand is hardly alone," Straub interjected.

"Your chain of command doesn't understand what you're
dealing with out here," Lin continued.

"If they don't, then I'm doing a terrible job in my
reports," Straub said. "And if that's the case, I'm going to be
real disappointed in myself."

Lin didn't speak for a moment. She pulled her hand out
from behind her back. In it was a datapad. She tossed it onto
Straub's desk. "I found Bendare."

Straub frowned. "Apparently I do have a problem with
expressing myself concisely and clearly."

"Bendare presents an ongoing problem for this station

outside the immediate scope of this particular investigation," Lin said. "I understand your direction, but as the head of security, I made a judgment call to ignore it in this instance."

Straub wagged a finger at her. "I see what you did there."

"I wasn't being subtle."

"No, you sure as hell weren't."

"Better to ask for forgiveness than permission."

"You keep saying that, yet I haven't heard you ask for any forgiveness yet." Straub picked up the datapad. "So where's Bendare?"

"Docking ring two, gate sixteen on the Festus vessel, the *Soul of Obsession*," Lin said.

"According to this they've been docked here for almost two weeks," Straub said.

"And Bendare hasn't so much as stepped off that ship," Lin said. "In fact, as I understand it, she occupies a section of the vessel that is located at the farthest point from the station itself. Five thousand, two hundred and eighty feet exactly."

20

_____

"I DON'T UNDERSTAND why we're here." Keane looked around the open lobby of the Church of Eternal Clarity. It was located on the highest level of the promenade, occupying a large space that, until recently, used to be home to the _Atlantic's_ second most popular hotel. The floors were white marble and the walls a soft beige. The end result was that the lobby was uncomfortably bright. The effect made Keane occasionally squint his eyes. He tried to stay focused on the handful of darker colors that were spread out among the lobby: the receptionist's desk, a few paintings, and the doors, solid black, that led to the rest of the Church.

"I had a run-in with this guy last night," Zemble said. He kept eyeing the receptionist suspiciously. She was an older woman with gray hair who seemed entirely disinterested in the fact that there were two UPA security officers sitting in her lobby.

"This guy?" Keane asked.

"Cavige," Zemble said. "The head of this cult."

Keane frowned. "I would hardly call this a cult."

Zemble looked at him, surprised. "Seriously?"

"I've seen cults," Keane said. "The Dzaferi on Kordal. They all committed ritual suicide after raping a group of women they had kidnapped from a small farming colony on their moon. The Trayvon are camped out on the third moon of Wyll and drink the urine of Tarupsani babies because they believe it gives them prophetic visions of the future and, coincidentally, all of these visions of the future have them living on this barren desert of a moon drinking cow piss for the rest of their lives. Or how 'bout the group of Marakis monks on starbase *Manhattan*? They all believe that if they live in the direct vicinity of the unfiltered radiation from the ion drives, they'll be immortal. They're also going to have tumors the size of their heads, but hey, they're immortal. So it's all a wash in the end."

Zemble just grunted wordlessly.

"Look, I'm willing to follow up on any leads you think you've got," Keane said. "But this?" He gestured at the receptionist and the doors. "There's no way this is a cult. And even if it was, this can't be anything related to Reynoso."

"Fizza had an appointment here," Zemble said. "In fact, according to his personal calendar he'd been coming here for the last three months."

Keane shrugged. "So?"

"Something about this place doesn't feel right," Zemble said. "I met this guy last night."

"You mentioned that already."

"My horns tingled."

Keane raised an eyebrow. "I'm sorry?"

"Something was off about him."

"And that made your horns tingle?"

Zemble shot him a look. "You try this every time."

"Because it sounds ridiculous every time."

"And yet, it's never been wrong."

Keane sighed. "Well, sure. I suppose. Still sounds stupid. Your tingling horns."

"Sounds stupid when you say it," Zemble grumbled.

"You should listen to yourself when you say it," Keane replied. "Sounds even worse." He folded his arms. "What exactly do you think we're going to find here? Hogle says Fizza killed himself."

"Maybe."

"I'm more worried about Reynoso potentially being poisoned," Keane said. "And, for that matter, so is Straub."

"I'm not convinced that Fizza isn't connected to this," Zemble said.

"Well, he's dead now. So his connection isn't going to be super helpful."

"Why'd he kill himself?"

"Because his boss was a degenerate," Keane said. "I'd want to kill myself, too, if I had to work for Reynoso."

"But Reynoso was already dead," Zemble said. "And Fizza knew that. If that was the case, he should have been happy."

"Who knows what he was feeling," Keane said. "Maybe it's a thin line between joy and depression in situations like this."

Zemble grunted. "Or maybe Fizza didn't kill himself."

"Maybe," Keane consented. "But this?" He gestured at the doors again.

"I did a little research on them," Zemble said. "They're one of the fastest growing religions in the UPA."

"Good for them."

Zemble looked at him.

"What?" Keane asked.

"They're crackpots."

Keane pointed to the doors. "They're crackpots?"

"They're essentially a power cult," Zemble said. "Most of their members are celebrities and power brokers. People with income at levels that only you and I dream of. Normal people can join, but they're typically given servant related roles within the organization. They believe psychiatry to be barbaric and inherently corrupt. Their sense of 'ethics' tends to be a sliding scale that basically tips in their favor, no matter whether it's right or wrong."

"And this makes them crackpots?"

Zemble looked at him, his face almost impassive. "No, specifically what makes them crackpots is that they believe that all sentient life in the galaxy was infected by immortal spirits called phetans and that these phetans are continuing to cause us spiritual harm on a daily basis."

"Sure. Because you believing in some omnipresent deity is sane and normal."

Zemble shrugged. "Well, I guess we'll find out who's right and who's wrong when we die and see who made it into Heaven."

Keane just stared at him for a second. "How the hell am I supposed to respond to that?"

"In addition," Zemble continued. "My faith doesn't require that we routinely brainwash new members."

"Agree to disagree on that point," Keane muttered under his breath.

"Okay, maybe this is something we can agree on: If you attempt to leave the Church, they've been known to completely destroy you."

"My gut says that you're being hyperbolic."

Zemble shook his head. "I came across multiple stories of individuals who left the church and then talked publicly about their experiences within it. These stories are almost always centered around forms of physical, emotional, mental or sexual abuse. The Church of Eternal Clarity responded with not only legal action, but also by revealing damaging secrets that had been discussed in the privacy of the church."

"Blackmail," Keane said.

Zemble nodded. "Blackmail."

"Okay, that sounds like it might have some relevance here," Keane said. "So if they're really this bad, what the hell are they doing out here on the *Atlantic* in one of the nicest pieces of property the station's got?"

Zemble didn't answer.

Keane snapped his fingers in Zemble's face. "Hello? You leaving something out here?"

Zemble folded his arms. "Much of the info I found on the Church of Eternal Clarity isn't...confirmed."

Keane sighed.

"They maintain a fairly legitimate front as just another alternative religion that's popular among the elite and celebrities," Zemble said quietly.

Keane closed his eyes for a second. "So what the hell are we doing here?"

"I met this guy last night," Zemble said.

"And your horns tingled."

"My horns tingled," Zemble repeated. "And I don't think Fizza killed himself."

"Your horns tingle at that, too?"

"As a matter of fact, yes," Zemble said. "I didn't mention it to you before because I knew how you were going to react and wanted to have something else to pair it with."

"Right." Keane folded his arms. "What's this guy's name again?"

"Joseph Michael Cavige."

Keane thought about it for a second. "I'll give you this."

"Yeah?"

"People who introduce themselves with their full name like that are never up to anything good."

"Thank you."

"Of course, that could just mean he's your typical religious leader fleecing his flock for his own financial good," Keane said.

Zemble grunted. "You know I pray for you every night."

"I wish you wouldn't."

"Which is why I make sure to do it every night."

"Even last night?"

"Especially last night," Zemble said.

"Because your horns tingled?"

"Exactly."

Keane shook his head.

The black doors opened and a tall, narrow man in a dark suit stepped out. He moved towards them with quick-footed grace. His face broke out into a wide grin as he reached for Zemble's hands.

"Lieutenant, somehow I knew I would see you again," Cavige said.

Zemble took one look at Cavige's outstretched hand and kept his arms folded.

Cavige chuckled softly and withdrew his hand. "Of course, that doesn't mean that I still don't have a little bit of work ahead of me."

Keane cleared his throat. "Mr. Cavige?"

Cavige easily pivoted from Zemble to Keane, his enthusiasm not wavering once. "Ah, yes. I was told the Lieutenant had brought a guest."

"I don't know that I would put it that way." Keane held out his hand. "Commander Cayden Keane from the *Defiance*."

"A pleasure to make your acquaintance," Cavige said, shaking his hand.

"I understand you've already met Lt. Zemble," Keane said.

"Zemble?" Cavige turned back to the hulking Elwat. "I certainly would have never guessed that in a thousand years."

Keane looked back and forth between them, confused.

Cavige chuckled softly again. "The lieutenant was rather closed off when we met last night. As such, he was reluctant to give me his name."

"Didn't seem relevant at the time," Zemble said. His voice sounded extra rumbly.

Cavige held out his hands, palms up. "And yet, here we are now. I think we both knew our meeting last night was not a coincidence. I don't know that I would go so far to call it divine providence, but..." He shrugged as he trailed off. "Zemble, though. I dare say that is quite an appropriate name for you. I believe it means 'gentle constant?'"

"You're familiar with Da'argh?" Zemble said, referring to the native language of his people.

Cavige tipped his hand side to side. "I dabble. I wouldn't say I'm fluent in it. There's a solid fifty-fifty chance your name could have been something else altogether and it would have gone right over my head. But it wasn't. So..." He shrugged again. "Makes you think."

Zemble grunted. "Sure. Okay."

Cavige smiled and gently wagged a finger at Zemble. "You are going to be a tough nut to crack, Mr. Zemble, but I think it's going to be worth it in the end."

"I'm not here for you to crack me open," Zemble said.

"Oh?" Cavige looked back and forth between them. "So

why are two security officers from the *Defiance* visiting my humble home today?"

"Imaad Fizza is a member of your congregation?" Keane asked.

Cavige took a breath before answering. It wasn't a particularly long pause, but there was something about it that caused Zemble's horns to tingle again. It was as if Cavige was gauging how much of the truth to share.

Slowly, Cavige nodded his head as he steepled his fingers. "Yes, Mr. Fizza is a member of my flock here. Is there a problem?"

"Well," Keane started.

Zemble cut him off. "He's dead."

Cavige blinked, his expression one of confusion and sadness. Zemble couldn't decide if the reaction was genuine or not.

"I beg your pardon?" Cavige asked.

"Fizza's dead," Zemble said again, with all the grace of an elephant stomping through the middle of a glass shop. "He was discovered this morning in his quarters, having hanged himself."

"Oh." Cavige's hand went to his chest as he took a step back as if in shock. "Oh."

Keane looked at Zemble, frowning with disapproval. Zemble didn't bother to return the look.

21

"We're sorry to have to break this to you like this," Keane said, working overtime to compensate for Zemble's borderline hostile attitude.

They sat in his office. It was subdued in comparison to the rest of the church and small to the point of almost being an afterthought.

Cavige leaned back in his chair, running his hand over his face. He looked every bit like a man who was having difficulty accepting a tragic bit of news.

Zemble didn't buy any of it.

"It's fine," Cavige said, sitting up. "I'm just...surprised."

"Are you?" Zemble asked.

Cavige looked at him, his face a mixture of confusion, grief and mild bemusement. "Yes, Lieutenant, as a matter of fact, I am. When Imaad first began attending our church, he was very much a broken man, trapped in a dark place. He was crying out for help and didn't even realize how loudly he was crying. I had been personally working with him over the last couple of months and I believe we had made several substantial breakthroughs and were in the process of rebuilding him. So, yes, to hear that he committed an act of suicide this morning, I am quite surprised. I thought things were better than that." He sighed. "Clearly I was wrong."

"There may be some extenuating circumstances to Fizza's death," Keane said, speaking just fast enough to keep Zemble from opening his mouth again.

Cavige looked at him, his eyes narrowed slightly, as if he was trying to conjure up a mental picture of whatever Keane was talking about. "What kind of circumstances?"

This time Keane didn't respond so fast. He took a moment, a brief moment, but a moment nonetheless. "This isn't public knowledge at this time, Mr. Cavige, so I would be very grateful if you kept this news to yourself for now."

Cavige nodded. "Of course."

"Ambassador Reynoso is dead," Keane said. "He died last night under suspicious circumstances."

"Ah." Cavige tilted his head back, an air of understanding coming down around him. "I see. Yes, okay." He paused and then asked, "May I ask what these circumstances were?"

"You may," Keane replied. "But I can't tell you without compromising the integrity of the investigation right now."

"Of course, that makes perfect sense." Cavige took a breath. "Well, gentlemen, this does cast everything into a different light."

"How so?" Keane asked.

Cavige paused. "I'll be honest with you, Commander, I'm not exactly sure how I should answer that."

"You could start with the truth," Zemble said.

Cavige gave Zemble a tired smile. "Mr. Zemble, I feel as though we got off on the wrong foot and no matter what I do, you won't let me help us onto the right foot."

"That's because I don't trust you," Zemble said.

Cavige adjusted himself in his seat, pressing his hands against his dark suit. "Well, that gets right to the heart of the matter."

Zemble leaned forward. "I think you're lying."

Cavige's eyes went wide with surprise. "About what?"

"Everything."

"That's pretty broad," Cavige said.

"Every time you open your mouth you seem to cover some pretty broad strokes," Zemble replied.

"And what exactly is this lack of trust based on?"

"It's a hunch."

"A hunch?" Cavige looked at Keane. "And do you share this hunch, Commander Keane?"

Keane gave Zemble a sharp look of disapproval before turning back to Cavige. "As a matter of fact, I don't. Please accept my apologies for the lieutenant's behavior. He's been having a difficult time lately."

Zemble growled. "I don't need you apologizing for me."

"Apparently you do," Keane said. "Otherwise you wouldn't be saying things that I need to be apologizing for. So why don't you just sit there and keep your mouth shut before you get into some real trouble."

Cavige raised his hand diplomatically. "Please, Commander, I'm not offended. I understand where Lieutenant Zemble is coming from. A man in his profession is naturally suspicious of everyone. It's what undoubtedly makes him such an excellent investigator." He looked at Zemble. "Just as a man in my position has to see the good in everyone, regardless of how they behave towards me."

"Hell of a compliment to pay a man who just accused you of lying to him," Keane said to Cavige, but he was looking at Zemble.

Cavige waved his hands with a sense of modest dismissiveness. "I am who I am."

"And who is that exactly?" Zemble asked. "Why would Fizza come to your church?"

"Because he clearly didn't have anywhere else to go," Cavige replied, unperturbed. "This station has an alarming lack of spiritual leadership."

"And why do you suppose that is?" Zemble asked.

"Obviously because when Pastor Loring left the *Atlantic*, there was no one to take his place," Cavige said. "The people felt lost and abandoned."

"And you just happened to be here to swoop in," Zemble said.

"You say it like it's a bad thing," Cavige replied.

"That's because from where I'm sitting it is."

"Ah." Cavige gestured for Zemble to switch seats with him. "Would you care to sit back here? Maybe you'll have a different point of view?"

Zemble didn't move from his seat.

"This may come as a surprise to you, Mr. Zemble, but I understand your hesitations," Cavige said.

"I doubt that," Zemble grumbled.

"Do you? Any man who accepts the sick and broken with open arms must clearly have an ulterior motive," Cavige said. "Who would do such a thing out of the goodness of their own heart?"

Zemble didn't respond.

"I believe you're familiar with a gentleman known as Jesus?" Cavige said. He had lowered his voice slightly.

"You're comparing yourself to the Son of God?" Zemble asked.

Cavige shrugged. "I'm just pointing out that where you

see suspicious behavior, I see the actions of an eternal savior."

"You're no Messiah," Zemble said.

"Of course not," Cavige agreed. "And I never said I was."

Zemble grunted wordlessly. He didn't need any words to convey his doubt.

"No, the problem here isn't telling you the truth," Cavige said, folding his hands on the surface of his desk as he brought them back on topic. "The problem lies within *what* I am *allowed* to tell you. While we certainly don't practice the Catholic's notions of confession, I do believe there is a sacred bond of trust between a man and his spiritual leader. Imaad shared things with me that weren't meant to be shared with others." He held up a hand as if they were about to protest. "Now, I understand that your argument is going to be that he's dead, but I don't necessarily believe that his death frees me from my promise of maintaining his confidence."

Keane looked at Zemble. The lieutenant didn't have anything to say. Although his expression was one of deep suspicion. Keane took a deep breath, rubbing his hands together as he turned back to Cavige. "That seems admirable. But we have to be practical here. Fizza's dead and even if you were his lawyer or his doctor, you would be free and clear, legally speaking, to share any information with us that you might think is relevant to the case.

"But I am neither a doctor nor a lawyer," Cavige said. "And I answer to a higher power than either of those professions do."

Zemble made a scoffing noise.

"Yes, Mr. Zemble?" Cavige asked. "You have a point to make?"

"Only that I find it amazing you just said that with a straight face," Zemble said.

"Lieutenant..." Keane warned in a low voice.

Zemble ignored him. "What higher power do you exactly believe in? Because as I understand it, the Church of Eternal Clarity doesn't believe in God."

"That doesn't mean we don't believe there's something greater than us," Cavige replied evenly.

"Would that be the phetans?" Zemble asked. "Or do they not count? Is there something greater than immortal spirits with malicious intents?"

Cavige's face grew stern. "This doesn't really seem like the time to defend the particulars of my faith to a nonbeliever."

"And why's that?" Zemble asked.

"Because you're supposed to be here about the death of Imaad Fizza," Cavige replied smoothly. "It would seem in poor taste to let ourselves get distracted by a theological discussion."

"I don't think he'll mind. He's dead," Zemble replied. "It's not like he's going to get any deader."

"Okay, that's *enough*, Lieutenant," Keane said, cutting back in.

Zemble grunted and settled back in his chair.

"Mr. Cavige," Keane said. "I respect your position." Beside him, Zemble made a loud scoffing sound. Keane shot him a quick look out of the corner of his eye and Zemble settled back into his chair like a pouting child. "But I've got a very short list of people that Reynoso was close enough to who could have some information regarding his death and at the top of that list is Imaad Fizza. But he's dead now and I can't really talk to him about this. So, if there's anything he might have mentioned to you over the last month that could even be remotely connected to this investigation, I would be very grateful if you would share it."

Cavige didn't speak for a few minutes. He stared at his hands, picking at his short nails.

Again, Zemble couldn't quite get a satisfactory read on Cavige. Everything about his behavior suggested a man who was genuinely struggling with how best to honor the wishes of a dead parishioner.

But something made his horns tingle.

Cavige looked up at both of them, his face somber and reflective. "What I would like both of you to understand is that Imaad Fizza was a deeply troubled young man."

"You mentioned that already," Zemble said impatiently.

Cavige nodded. "And I mention it again in an attempt to drive home the point. He first graced our doors almost exactly five months ago. At first glance, he was tired, stressed and overwhelmed past his natural breaking point. Naturally, most people would have attributed this to his position as aide to Ambassador Reynoso. But I wasn't aware of his job when I first met Imaad. So when I met him, all I saw was a young man who was so far past his breaking point, it was a wonder he was even still standing.

"Like most who come to our doors, Imaad wasn't sure what he was looking for. He wasn't even aware that he was looking for anything. But we're all searching for something, some of us just happen to be more in tune with the notion that we're lost. And as I mentioned to you last night, Mr. Zemble, I like to believe there's more than one way to seek guidance in this vast universe of ours."

"You can skip the sales pitch," Zemble said. "Neither of us are interested in joining your cult."

"Cult?" Cavige echoed in mild disbelief.

"That is *enough*, Lieutenant," Keane snapped. "Maybe you need to wait outside while I finish this interview."

Zemble growled. "Commander-"

"It's not up for debate," Keane said. "It was a politely worded order."

Zemble got to his feet.

"Please, Commander Keane," Cavige said. "I would like Mr. Zemble to stay."

Keane looked at him in surprise. "You would?"

Cavige nodded. "As I already told you, I'm not easily offended. I understand that Mr. Zemble has plenty of reservations about our church. It's perfectly natural. Questions are part of who we are in this universe. If we didn't have questions, we wouldn't be the people we are." He gestured to Zemble's empty seat. "Imaad had questions, too. Questions he wasn't even aware of."

Cavige paused, waiting for Zemble to resume his seat. When he didn't, Cavige simply shrugged and continued on unperturbed.

"My first interaction with Imaad was immediately after his first service. I like to stand near the exit and speak with anyone who's looking for a friendly voice to talk to, at least for a few minutes. Imaad wasn't interested in talking. He had a dazed look about him and he would have left without a single word had I not stopped him."

"Why'd you stop him?" Keane asked.

Cavige shrugged, holding up his hands in the classic pose of I-don't-know. "I couldn't really tell you. Sometimes you just get a feeling in your gut."

For the briefest of moments, Cavige's gaze flicked back to Zemble. It was timed with the blink of his eyes so it was hardly even noticeable. But Zemble noticed it and, even more, he believed that Cavige wanted him to notice it.

"We didn't talk for long," Cavige continued. "Just a few minutes. Just long enough for me to see how desperately this young man was crying out for help. I convinced him to come by the following day so we could have a longer one-on-one session. He seemed hesitant at the notion and, honestly, I wasn't sure he was even going to show. I make this offer to many people every day and as Mr. Zemble here can attest, many of them, if not most of them, are less than inclined to take advantage of my offer.

"But the next day came and much to my surprise, there Imaad was. It was a short meeting; we didn't talk about much. He mentioned he worked for Ambassador Reynoso and I commented on how that must be a stressful job. Imaad laughed at that. It was during our later meetings that we began to uncover some...truths he had suppressed over the years." Cavige paused again, visibly uncertain as to whether or not he should continue. He took a deep, centering breath and then said, "Imaad was abused as a child. We believe that it was his father, but it's been difficult to pinpoint exactly who the abuser was or even the nature of the abuse."

"That seems...a little unusual," Keane said.

"Yes and no. You see, Imaad wasn't even consciously aware of this trauma," Cavige said. "It had been suppressed deep within his psyche. The only way we were able to uncover portions of it was through assaying."

"Assaying?" Keane repeated.

"Obviously I'm not going to get into the particulars of the technique, but simply put: it's the process of gaining clarity," Cavige explained. "It's something every member of our church must go through. It's an ongoing process as clarity is something we must each strive for every day. However, in the case of newer members, such as Imaad, the process can be more intense as we have to dig through decades of calcified experiences that have created a thick, almost impenetrable barrier around their psyche's soul. There are things within each of us that we forget over time. Not because we try to, not because we're forced to, simply because we just do. Time doesn't heal all wounds; it just patches them over year by year."

"Sounds an awful lot like therapy," Keane said

"On the surface, yes, perhaps. But I assure you, the differences between the two are as vast as the gulf of distance between the ends of our galaxy," Cavige said. "Over our sessions we discovered the nature of his relationship with Ambassador Reynoso and how it related to the abuse he had suffered as a child. Slowly, but surely, we were healing him. The last time I saw him, just two days ago, he was the happiest I had ever seen him.

"So yes, to hear that he took his own life, I do find very troubling."

"What exactly did he say about Ambassador Reynoso?" Keane asked.

The question seemed to catch Cavige off guard. "I'm sorry?"

"You mentioned that the two of you were discussing the nature of his relationship with Reynoso," Keane said. "What exactly did he say about Reynoso?"

Cavige appeared to think for a moment. "Well, he spoke about Reynoso with a sense of respect."

"Respect?" Keane echoed in mild disbelief.

"Yes. Well, often that respect was laced with disgust and revulsion," Cavige said. "According to Imaad, the ambassador was a complicated man."

"That's certainly one way of describing him," Keane said.

"I never had the opportunity to personally meet him myself," Cavige said. "All I know of him is what Imaad told me."

"And what did Imaad tell you?"

Cavige tilted his head to the side. "Is there something specific you're looking for, Commander?"

"Honestly, I don't know," Keane admitted. "But I imagine I would know it if I heard it."

Cavige chuckled softly again. "Yes. That gut feeling. Imaad talked about Reynoso much like he talked about his father: one moment he would praise him and the next he would curse him. He believed that the ambassador was a great man who had fallen prey to even greater sins."

"Did Fizza ever talk about bringing Reynoso here?" Zemble asked.

"As a matter of fact, he did," Cavige said. "He thought that I might be able to help the ambassador the same way that I helped him."

"And did you?" Keane asked.

Cavige shook his head. "No. He never brought the ambassador by."

"Maybe that's a good thing," Zemble said.

"How so?" Cavige asked.

"Fizza killed himself after receiving your help."

Cavige's face darkened. "I am a patient man, Lieutenant. But my patience has *limits*."

"Of course, Reynoso ended up dead as well," Zemble continued. "So maybe you helped him after all."

Keane got to his feet. "That is *way* over the line, Lieutenant," he snapped.

"Commander, I think we're done here," Cavige said, getting up.

Keane glared at Zemble for an extra second before

turning back to Cavige. "Yeah, that sounds pretty reason-able." He paused, clearing his throat. "Again, I want to apol-ogize for Lieutenant Zemble's behavior."

Cavige tilted his head forward slightly. "Apology accepted."

Keane exhaled a brief sigh of relief.

"But," Cavige continued. "I believe I will need to file an official complaint."

There was a heavy silence in the office that seemed to drop upon the two Defiance officers like a lead blank.

Keane pressed his lips together, struggling to keep a neutral expression. His hands hung at his sides, fingers twitching, as if they wanted to do something and weren't sure what it was they wanted to do. "Of course," he said, his voice sounding slightly strained. "That's...perfectly under-standable."

"I don't enjoy being accused of murder," Cavige said.

"Neither would I," Keane replied, his voice sounding more strained.

"But it's more than that." Cavige looked at Zemble. "It's nothing personal, Mr. Zemble. But I am a strong believer in teachable moments and despite your behavior towards me, I still want you to be the best version of you that you can be. You clearly have, for lack of a better word, a problem. Some-thing has poisoned you right to your soul and I don't think you realize that." His gaze softened with something that appeared to be genuine concern. "And, worse, I don't think you *want* to realize that. My goal with this complaint is to help you, not hurt you. I hope that, with time and, more importantly, the necessary work, you'll come to understand that."

Zemble grunted, unimpressed. "If your help is going to leave me in the same position as Fizza, I'll pass."

Keane's fingers figured out what they wanted to do and curled into fists. He forced them to uncurl. "Okay, thank you for your time, Mr. Cavige." He started pushing Zemble towards the door before he could accuse Cavige of anything else. "We'll see ourselves out."

22

"HE'S LYING," Zemble said once they were on the open promenade.

"What the *hell* is *wrong* with you?" Keane snapped.

Zemble looked back at the Church of Eternal Clarity. "I don't think he was surprised to learn that Fizza was dead. I think half of what he told us about how he and Fizza met was made up on the spot. I think he knew who Fizza was working for before he ever approached Fizza. And I think he was definitely using Fizza to get to Reynoso."

Keane clapped his hands in Zemble's face. "Hey, are you *listening* to me?"

Zemble slowly turned back to Keane. "Yes, I'm listening to you. The problem is *you're* not listening to *me*. This is our guy."

"You were way out of line back there," Keane said.

Zemble stared at him for a second, as if confused. "I was following a lead."

"You straight up accused that man of a *double homicide*."

"If that's all he gets charged with he's getting off lucky," Zemble said. "He's probably complicit in a lot more deaths.

What would he have said if we asked to speak with some of the other members of his congregation?"

"After you accused him of *murder*? He probably wouldn't have warmed up to the idea," Keane said.

"Sure," Zemble said. "But not because of that."

"Oh my goodness," Keane muttered. "You haven't been listening to a single damn word I've said."

"Because most of what you've said is just you whining."

"*Hey!*" Keane barked at him. "You're clearly not getting that you're on the receiving end of the shit stick here. Do you realize what just happened back there? We're supposed to be handling this investigation with *discretion*. How in the hell are you being discreet when you're getting a damn complaint filed against you?"

Zemble didn't say anything to that.

Keane nodded. "Okay, so you are listening to me."

Zemble started for the nearest lift.

"Where the hell do you think you're going, Lieutenant?" Keane snapped at him.

Zemble stopped and turned back. "I thought you were done."

Keane held up both of his hands. "I am *far* from done."

"What else do you have to say that hasn't already been said?" Zemble asked. "You publicly reprimanded me. Cavige's going to file a complaint. I don't see how there's anything further to be gained from discussing this right now."

"Well, for starters, I clearly need to get it through your thick skull how badly you screwed up back there."

Zemble shrugged. "The man's a cult leader and most likely a murderer. There are worse people to insult."

"It's like you've suddenly forgotten how to run a damn investigation."

Zemble pointed at him. "And it's like you've suddenly forgotten how to trust my instincts."

"Your instincts led us to an admittedly kooky church and a guy whose biggest sin seems to be thinking he's the next galactic messiah," Keane said.

"You can't be serious."

"I am *very* serious."

Zemble folded his arms. "You mean to tell me you sat through that entire interview and you didn't hear a single thing that set off any alarm bells for you?"

"Oh, I heard several things," Keane said. "Most of them came from your mouth."

Zemble growled at him.

Keane jabbed a finger at him. "Don't you start that shit with me. You walked in there and treated Cavige like he was guilty from the word *go*. Everything you said put him on the defensive. So, yeah, everything that came out of his mouth sounded a little off. Would he have sounded like that if you hadn't been in there? Maybe, maybe not."

"This is bullshit. You know there's something off with him."

"Yeah, I also know that thanks to your song and dance back there, if we do find he's connected to this at all, guess what's going to be the first thing his lawyer drops in front of the judge to get the whole case thrown out?" Keane pointed at Zemble. "*You.*"

Again, Zemble didn't have anything to say.

Keane took a calming breath and ran a hand through his hair. He took a step back and leaned against the wall. After a few seconds, Keane said, "Look you're absolutely right, something's definitely off about him. Could be he's up to his neck in whatever this is. Could be he's just a dirtbag who's using his made-up religion to take advantage of people. I don't know. What I do know is that I had enough presence of mind not to go after him without at least *something* to back me up. That's something you used to be really good at. You want me to give your tingling horns credit? I'll give 'em credit. When you get a hunch, it's usually a pretty solid hunch. It's why I asked the captain to bring you in on Directive Fifty-Two. You are a solid, reliable investigator. But your tingling horns don't amount to anything if they don't actually lead to *something*. And they didn't lead to anything before we got here and they sure as hell didn't lead to anything in there."

Zemble avoided his gaze and stared down at the floor.

Keane exhaled, rubbing his hands over his face. "I didn't get any sleep last night either."

Zemble looked up at him. "Sorry?"

"I spent the night out drinking with Nax and Warrick. Ended it in the quarters of a young lady whose name I do not remember and after some activities that definitely did not include sleep, I did eventually fall asleep. And less than three hours later Captain Mitchell called me in on this case." He held out his arms. "Look at me."

"I'm looking at you."

"You'd never know that was the night I had."

"Is there a point to this? Or are you bored of yelling at me so you thought you'd try bragging about yourself for a few minutes?" Zemble asked.

Keane dropped his arms. "I know I'm the kettle calling the pot black, but there's definitely been something off with you and whatever it is isn't just because you're not getting a good night's sleep." When Zemble didn't say anything, Keane said, "I know you've been spending a lot of time with Calloway."

Zemble looked him with a deadpan expression. "Is that a problem?"

Keane met his gaze and shrugged. "I don't know. You tell me. Your neighbors tell me you haven't spent more than twenty minutes in your quarters since we docked here."

"It's been nice to stretch my legs on the *Atlantic*," Zemble replied.

"According to the logs yesterday was the first day you stepped off the ship," Keane said. "We've been here for two weeks."

"Where is this line of questioning supposed to go?"

"I don't know," Keane admitted. "But I figure I'll know it when I get there."

"You don't want to talk to me about this," Zemble said.

"And yet here I am, talking with you about it."

Before Zemble could respond, Keane's communicator buzzed with a message. He glanced at it and pushed off from the wall. "Straub has a lead on Bendare."

"Let's go." Zemble started for the lift again.

"Oh, hell, no," Keane said. "You're not going anywhere near Bendare right now. The last thing I need is for you to start accusing her of murder. She's not going to stop at filing a complaint. She'll bury our ship and the whole station." He shook his head. "No, you're going back to the *Defiance*."

"What the hell am I supposed to do there?"

"I don't know. Reflect on your actions. Take a nap. Hell, you can pray for all I care. Do whatever. As if this moment, you're not on this case."

23

KEANE AND STRAUB stood side by side in front of the closed doors.

Like most of the docking gates on the *Atlantic* the portal had a diameter of ten feet. The doors themselves were a drab grey and the circular border surrounding them was a bold red. In the center, painted in the same bold red was the number 16.

The rest of the gate was empty.

It was just Straub and Keane standing there, waiting for the doors to open.

Keane clasped his hands behind his back and rocked back on his heels. "I'm not going to lie, I'm a little confused as to why you're here."

Straub rubbed her left temple. "Bendare is...complicated. She doesn't like meeting new people. Especially if those new people are here to ask her questions about her connection to a recently deceased ambassador."

"And you think she'll respond better to you?" Keane asked. "The woman who kicked her off the station under some broadly defined indecency law?"

"I figure she's less likely to shoot you if I'm here."

Both of Keane's eyebrows went up at them. "Should I be armed?"

"No, that'll only make things worse."

Keane looked around, noting again how it was just the two of them. "Should there maybe be a few more officers here then?"

Straub shook her head. "No, that'll just make her feel like she's getting ganged up on."

Keane turned back to the closed doors. "Oh, this is going to be fun."

"It's certainly going to be something," Straub agreed. "Where's Lieutenant Zemble again?"

"Following up another lead," Keane replied diplomatically.

"Related to this Cavige character?"

"Something like that."

"Why do I not like the sound of that?"

"Probably because you have an excellent ear for bull-shit," Keane said.

Straub gave him a small smile. "Commander, are you trying to flatter me?"

He returned the smile. "Depends on if it's working?"

The smile dropped from her face so fast Keane wondered if it had ever been there to begin with. "It's not. So cut the shit."

Keane cleared his throat awkwardly. "Yes, ma'am."

Another few seconds of awkward silence passed and the doors still didn't open.

"Is there a bell we're supposed to ring?" Keane asked.

"Nope."

"We're just supposed to wait here?"

"Well, we don't exactly have probable cause to just barge in," Straub said. "So, yes. We're just supposed to wait here."

"Sounds like a real petty power move."

"Obviously she's still a little pissed at me."

Keane scratched the back of this head. "You used to serve under Captain Mitchell."

Straub folded her arms. "Yep."

"What was that like?"

She looked at him. "What do you mean?"

Keane shrugged. "I mean, I guess you served with him before, you know, Directive Fifty-Two and everything."

She turned back to the door. "Here's a tip, Commander."

"Yeah?"

"Don't talk about a top secret government agency while we're standing outside the front of a ship belonging to a notorious black-market arms dealer and blackmailer."

"Right. That sounds like something I probably should have thought of on my own."

"Yep."

Another minute of awkward silence passed.

"Seriously, though," Keane said. "You served under Mitchell."

"Yeah."

Keane raised his eyebrows expectantly.

She sighed. "There has to be something you're looking for."

"Honestly, I think I'm just trying to make small talk," he admitted.

"Stop it," she said. "With any luck, I won't even have to talk to you again after today."

"Yes, ma'am." Keane turned back to the doors. "You really don't want me here right now, do you?"

"Nope."

"You'd probably prefer Commander Lin."

"Yep."

"Because this is a thing the two of you started."

"Yep."

"You know, I'd like to think I'm a pretty solid investigator," Keane said.

Straub didn't say anything.

"I mean, I'm at least as good as Lin," Keane continued. He looked down at his legs. "Of course, I don't have her legs." He caught Straub looking at him sideways. "I'll just stand here quietly now."

"That would be appreciated."

There was a soft hiss and the doors finally slid open. On the other side stood a tall, gray-skinned Vulderran, dressed in a dark grey suit with a heavy black overcoat. He stood at a hair or two just over seven feet and his frame was thick and muscular. Thanks to a thick brow that extended just over his eyes and flat, almost squashed nose, his face appeared to be frozen in a permanent scowl. Atop his head was a black hat with a narrow brim and a yellow feather. Jutting out from the open flap of his overcoat was the butt of an intimidatingly large fusion pistol that sat in a holster under his left arm.

For a long minute, Keane was almost certain the Vulderran was going to shoot them on the spot. He wasn't entirely certain why he thought this. Such an act would have terrible consequences for everyone involved: Keane and Straub would be dead. The Vulderran would be arrested, or more likely killed while resisting arrest. There would be some kind of political fallout with the Vulder government. At the very least the UPA would issue some kind of sanction against them. Bendare herself would have a hard time twisting her way out of being connected to the death of a high ranking UPA official. There could even be some kind of prolonged engagement here on the station, threatening the lives of many of the people occupying the *Atlantic*. It would be disastrous.

And yet, the look on the Vulderran's face made Keane feel all but certain that he was going to pull out his fusion pistol and blow a hole out the back of each of their heads.

Keane, momentarily forgetting he wasn't running the show at this particular moment, opened his mouth, starting to say something, but not entirely certain what he was going to say.

But before Keane could say anything, the Vulderran spoke. "Commodore, as always, it is a delight to see you." His accent reminded Keane of characters from old Twentieth Century films that took place in the seedy underbelly of London.

Straub frowned. "Jacoby. You look...alive and well."

The Vulderran smiled. "Why thank you. I recently started a new diet and I think it not only agrees with my health, but also my mental state of mind."

"Good for you," Straub replied flatly.

Jacoby clapped his hands together. The noise they made was like two pieces of wet cement smacking against each other. "Well now, I think the two of you have waited long enough. So why don't we get on with it."

Without waiting for any kind of response Jacoby turned and started walking.

Keane and Straub looked at each other and then quickly followed after him.

"There are rules," the Vulderran said as they continued down the corridor. Like most Festusian ships everything was built wide and over-lit. The corridor would have easily accommodated three Elwats the size of Zemble side-by-side and there still would have been room for a small child to walk in step with them. "Now, of course, Commodore Straub is already familiar with these rules, so this is for your benefit, Commander Keane. Please do me the courtesy of paying attention and remembering the rules. Rule One: Do not touch her."

Straub snorted contemptuously.

Jacoby looked back at her. "If you think you're going to have difficulty with these rules, then I would recommend you leave now and return to the *Atlantic*."

"Your ship is still docked at my station," she replied.

"That may be," he agreed. "But you'll find that Ms. Bendare is adhering very closely to the guidelines you set regarding her presence."

"Fancy way of saying she's afraid of trespassing onto the station," Straub said.

Jacoby stopped and turned to face her with his full attention. There was a cold expression on his face. "You would do well to keep in mind that Ms. Bendare is not afraid of you or your rule of law. She is simply providing you the respect your position presumably deserves. She asks that you simply do the same for her." His expression softened. "Now, do you believe this will be a problem for you?"

Straub gritted her teeth and kept her hands behind her back, where Jacoby couldn't see her yanking at her fingers in frustration. "Not. At. All," she said with forced pleasantness.

A wide grin broke out on Jacoby's face. "Excellent." He turned and resumed leading them down the corridor. "Now then, Rule Number Two: Please do not use foul language in Ms. Bendare's presence. She finds that kind of vulgar language distasteful, disturbing and offensive."

"Well, shit," Keane said.

Jacoby shot him a look over his shoulder.

"Just getting it out of my system now," Keane said, smirking.

"Rule Number Three." Jacoby stopped in front of a closed double door. He pressed his hand against a pad next to it and after a second the doors slid open. Like the previous corridor, this one was wide and lit from above and below. Stepping through the door Jacoby picked up his pace slightly. "And this is the most important of the rules, at least in my opinion. Do not yell. Do not raise your voice beyond what would be considered a normal level of volume for a casual conversation."

"So far this has the feeling of anything but," Keane said.

Jacoby nodded. "I imagine so. Which is why these rules exist. Things can become...*intense* in Ms. Bendare's presence."

"Intense," Keane echoed as Jacoby took them around a wide corner.

The floor beneath them began to slope upwards gently. It was nearly a full thirty seconds before Straub realized the minor effort she was making as she walked.

"Ms. Bendare has found, over the years, that people have certain opinions about her," Jacoby explained. "These opinions, whether valid or not, tend to color an individual's perceptions of her before they ever have a chance to meet with her face to face. And, more often than not, preconceived perceptions of Ms. Bendare are rather negative."

"I wonder where she could have possibly developed such a reputation," Straub said flatly.

"Indeed," Jacoby agreed.

Keane couldn't tell if he was being sincere or not.

They approached another set of doors and Jacoby brought them to a standstill as he tapped the call button.

"It'll be just a few more minutes," he explained.

There was a low humming noise from the other side of the doors and then they felt a brief jolt underneath their feet. The doors slid open revealing a glass-enclosed horizontal lift.

Jacoby stepped to the side and held out his arm gesturing for them to enter. "After you, please."

Jacoby followed them into the lift and tapped in a destination on the control panel. A moment later, they started moving.

Through the clear glass around them Keane had a view of an open space, possibly even large enough to house the *Defiance* in its entirety. Instead of the typical trappings of a starship, it was filled with what appeared to an entire alien forest.

Keane moved closer to one of the windows for a better look. "Wow."

Jacoby stood next to the doors, his arms clasped behind his back. "It is a sight to behold. No one makes ships quite like the Festus. Every single one of their vessels is equipped with a terrarium like this. They believe that it's necessary to bring a little bit of their home with them every time they head out into the stars."

Keane pressed a hand against the window. "I had heard rumors, but I never imagined it would be anything like this."

"Well, the *Soul of Obsession* is a bit unique," Jacoby explained. "It is one of the largest in their fleet. Most Festus vessels only have a terrarium about a quarter of this. Usually less. Just enough for them to retire to on a regular basis to help reset their biological clocks. The *Soul of Obses-*

sion here is unique as it is not intended to return back to their home world for another fifteen years."

Keane looked back at him, surprised. "That's a hell of a long time."

Jacoby's gaze narrowed. "Language, please." His expression relaxed back into that casual scowl that Keane now realized was just his natural resting face. "Yes, I'll grant you it is an unusually long period of time. But that is the period of time that Ms. Bendare has contracted the use of this vessel for."

"The entire ship?" Keane asked, surprised. "She's renting the *entire* ship?"

Jacoby nodded. "Ms. Bendare does not like to share."

Keane turned back to the terrarium below. "No kidding."

"Ms. Bendare also has very specific accommodation requests that only the Festus have been able to meet for her," Jacoby continued. "Most starships, despite their size, are built in such a way that feels claustrophobic. Considering your current assignment, Commander Keane, I would imagine you understand that perfectly."

Keane turned back to him, again, surprised.

"Please don't be so surprised," Jacoby said. "Ms. Bendare has a full dossier prepared on everyone who comes to see her. It helps even the playing field, as it were. That's just good business."

"And what exactly is in that file?" Keane asked.

Jacoby paused for a moment, recalling the broad strokes of the report. "Well, as I understand it, you overcame quite the crippling medical event."

Keane stared at him for a moment, trying to figure out if Jacoby was being sarcastic or not. He decided he didn't care. He turned back to the view outside the window. "So

Bendare likes Festus ships because they're built to feel roomy."

"Exactly," Jacoby continued. "Roomy. I like that word. *Roomy*. Feels exactly like what it's describing. Space doesn't agree with Ms. Bendare. It doesn't feel right, as it were. It's her belief, and if we're being honest, mine as well, we don't really belong out here. It's not *natural*. She doesn't like to be reminded that the only thing between her and the cold void of the outside is about twenty feet of whatever your preferred material is for starship construction. That's one of the reasons she enjoyed the space of the *Atlantic*. It didn't feel claustrophobic. Helped her feel like she was on an actual planet. She was rather heartbroken when you had her removed, Commodore."

Straub folded her arms and pointedly didn't look outside the window. "Right. Heartbroken."

The terrarium below them disappeared as the lift slid into a metal shaft and then a moment later came to a stop.

"Ah, here we are." Before he opened the doors he addressed both of them with a solemn expression. "Now do please keep in mind the three rules. While you both seem to be in relatively reasonable moods, I will not hesitate to take action against you for violating any of them."

"Is that supposed to be a threat?" Straub asked.

"Not at all," Jacoby said. "I like to think you know better than that, Commodore. I don't believe in threats." He held out his hands, palms up. "I'm simply reminding you of your current circumstances. You see, once you step off this lift you are no longer within the confines of the trespassing order. You no longer have any legal authority to take any action against Ms. Bendare. In fact, there is one more reason Ms. Bendare is so fond of Festus ships: They are among the few ships that operate with impunity within the Alliance.

Thanks to the addition of the terrariums on every vessel, each ship is treated, legally speaking, as an extension of the Festus home planet. And, as such, the powers afforded to you as a member in good standing with the UPA Fleet are extremely limited while onboard our ship here."

Behind him the doors slid open and Jacoby stepped to the side again, gesturing for them to step off with a polite, if slightly disturbing grin. "Now, if you're ready, Ms. Bendare will see you."

24

ZEMBLE DID NOT GO BACK to the *Defiance*.

He started to go back. His first instinct had been to simply do as ordered and just return. Despite his frustration with Keane, he understood where he had gone wrong, and Keane was right in sending him back. So he started to go back to the ship.

Except, he wasn't sure what he was going to do back on the *Defiance*. He felt like he couldn't go back to Calloway's room, not after both Rabkin and Keane had called him out on it. But had they, though? They had simply taken notice of the obvious, of what literally anyone with the ability of sight would have seen. It wasn't like he was being sneaky about it. In fact, it was nearly impossible for Zemble to be sneaky onboard the *Defiance*. He certainly had the ability to be discreet, but between his large stature and the almost claustrophobic design of the ship, it was nearly impossible for him to be sneaky. And what would he have to be sneaky about? He was simply visiting a friend in need.

But regardless, he felt like he couldn't go back to

Calloway's room. Not that she would have anything to offer him by way of advice or direction.

And he didn't want to go back to his quarters. His quarters felt even worse. At least with Calloway he felt vaguely at home like he wasn't someplace completely alien to him.

So what would he even do back at the *Defiance*? Sit around in the commissary waiting for Cavige's complaint to come through? That seemed like an extraordinarily bad idea. Maybe he could reach out to Captain Mitchell and get ahead of the complaint? Surely the captain would understand the situation? But that felt like an even worse idea. Zemble was not a person who 'got ahead' of things like that. It was going to be whatever it was going to be and he would deal with it when the time came.

Except he needed to do something because if he wasn't doing something he couldn't distract himself from the other *thing*. That absence of pain that kept nagging at him, like an irritating itch at the center of his back that he couldn't reach He knew he had to deal with it, but he didn't know how to. So instead he needed something to distract him.

Cavige.

His mind latched onto Cavige's smug, holier-than-thou face.

Cavige.

He briefly entertained the idea of going back to Cavige and punching him in the face. After all, he was already going to file a complaint on Zemble, so Zemble might as well actually do something worthy of a complaint.

But the saner part of his mind quickly prevailed, talking him out of that particular bad idea.

Still, there was something about Cavige.

It was odd that he had run into Cavige the night before

and then had this case that was connected to Cavige now. It was...

Zemble paused.

What was it exactly?

An obvious answer poked at the back of his mind: Divine providence.

He wasn't a fan of the concept. It was too easy to prescribe things that seemed coincidental or beneficial to God. Because what happened when those things didn't work out? Or what happened when there was no coincidental connection to highlight something important? Did that mean God simply took the day off?

(But then why did God let Steve send him to that place?)

Zemble shook his head. It was a slippery slope. Sometimes a coincidence was just a coincidence.

Of course, just because he was having difficulty talking to God didn't mean God was going to have any difficulty talking to him. And he was hard-pressed to come up with any other explanation as to why Cavige was suddenly in his orbit a good twelve hours before he got this case.

He let the notion stew, focusing on it for a moment before letting it slide to the back of his mind for his subconscious to work on.

Regardless, there was a problem with Cavige. He knew it. Keane even knew it. Maybe the problem with Cavige wasn't related to Reynoso and Fizza's death, but Zemble doubted that.

At some point, without even consciously realizing it, he found himself back at Fizza's quarters.

Staring at the closed doors he tried to retrace his steps in his mind, figure out the series of mental events that led him back here and found he couldn't quite piece them together.

There was nothing on the door indicating the scene was

sealed off. Due to the sensitive nature of the investigation Fizza's quarters were simply sealed under a security lock. As far as they could tell, Fizza had no close friends on the station who needed to be notified about his passing. In fact, outside of his connection to Cavige, Fizza didn't seem to have any sign of life on the station beyond working for Reynoso.

Something nagged at the back of Zemble's mind. It had taken up residence next to the notion of God directing him into this investigation in the first place: It was Cavige's unspoken suggestion that Fizza had killed himself because of the resurfacing memories of his abuse. Except that didn't ring true for Zemble. If everything Cavige was saying was true, he was really helping Fizza and Fizza didn't seem to be in any denial of this. In fact, according to Cavige, it seemed as though Fizza was grateful for Cavige's help.

So then why wouldn't Fizza have reached out to Cavige before hanging himself?

Zemble stared at the sealed doors, the question playing itself in a loop, over and over again through his mind. He reached out and tapped in the override code. The doors slid open and Zemble stepped inside. A moment later the doors slid closed behind him.

There was a smell of death in the air.

Zemble knew that wasn't true. The *Atlantic's* air recycling system ran on a triple purification structure. They hadn't even smelled Fizza's corpse when it was present. It didn't matter, though. His brain told him there was a smell of death there and he wasn't going to argue with it.

"Lights to full," Zemble said. His voice sounded surprisingly coarse to him.

Around him light slowly flared up, illuminating Fizza's living quarters and chasing away the dark shadows that tugged at the portions of his subconscious that were still afraid of things that went bump in the night.

The light helped a little with the death smell, but not by much.

Fizza's quarters were a mess. Most of the mess had been caused, presumably, by Fizza. Zemble didn't like that. Everything he had heard about the man suggested he wasn't the kind of person to live in a garbage dump. So why did his quarters look like one?

Zemble glanced in the direction of where they had found Fizza's dangling body, but his instincts told him there wasn't going to be anything there.

(Instincts? Or something else? Maybe a little voice at the back of his mind that he was having difficulty hearing? The Holy Spirit?)

Zemble shook his head to clear out the thoughts. God wasn't an amateur detective who spent His time passing along clues to the professionals on murder investigations.

(He should really give God a little more credit than that. After all, He was God. Wasn't He supposed to be interested in the big and small? The micro and the macro? The problems of the galaxy and the problems of one man? He was Almighty and omniscient, of course He could spare the time. And really, if the Almighty wanted to help out with a murder investigation, who was he to turn down the help?)

Zemble grunted out loud and made his way through the mess, careful not to touch anything. Clothes, books, and random objects were cluttered across the floor. The sofa had a pile of what appeared to be dirty laundry on it and Fizza's desk, located in the farthest corner of the room, was covered in papers and datapads.

He wasn't sure what he was looking for, but as Keane had said, he'd probably know it when he found it.

Zemble picked up one of the datapads and thumbed it on. It was work-related. Messages and appointments for Reynoso stretching back for the last month and then ahead for the next two months. He tossed it back on the desk and made his way to Fizza's bedroom.

Here everything was a little more organized. There was still a mess, but there seemed to be a purpose to the mess. There was a suitcase on the bed and piles of clothes around it. The code was easy enough to crack: Fizza had clearly been preparing for a sudden trip.

Fizza had been thinking about running.

In Zemble's mind, two pieces clicked together.

He moved over to the nightstand on the left side of the bed. He ignored the one on the right. Everything on the bed, the pillows, the blanket, they leaned left. Fizza didn't spend any time on the other side of his bed. So, logically, if there was anything he was looking for, it would be in the left-hand nightstand.

And what was he looking for?

Zemble still didn't have an answer to that. At least, he didn't think he did.

He hooked his thumb under the handle of the top drawer and slid it out. There was one book in it: The Clarity of Sacred Scripture.

"Of course," Zemble muttered.

He picked up the leather-bound book and flipped through it. A handful of words and passages jumped out at him. Phrases that seemed out of place and yet almost too perfectly placed. After a few minutes of skipping through it, his head started to ache. He closed the book and set it down on the surface of the nightstand.

Zemble stared at the book for a minute, another piece clicking in his mind. With every passing second, his headache became less. He suspected that if he were to pick up the book and start flipping through it again, the headache would return.

(The Lord works in mysterious ways.)

"Yes He does," Zemble agreed out loud.

He closed the top drawer and opened the bottom one.

Here he found another datapad. He thumbed it on and the screen lit up with a message: USER NOT AUTHORIZED.

Zemble glance down at his thumb. The datapad was obviously keyed to Fizza's biometrics.

The datapad in the living room, however, the one that had months of sensitive data regarding the ambassador's schedule had been left unlocked without any kind of security on it.

So what made this one so special?

Zemble flipped the datapad over. Keane knew tricks for getting pass security lockouts like this. But he doubted Keane would be likely to offer him any help right now if he reached out to him. Instead, Zemble fell back on a piece of training he learned back during his first assignment.

Biometric security was the most secure. It was nearly impossible to duplicate a DNA scan, a facial scan or even a simple iris scan. It was often the default form of security for most private individuals. Within the Fleet, however, most sensitive programs were locked by a combination passcode/biometric lock. The logic being that even if you could spoof one, it would be impossible to spoof both. What most private individuals didn't realize, though, was that if you didn't bother with a passcode setting, it would simply default to the factory security code. Of course, you still had to get past the biometric portion of the lock.

Zemble popped open the lower panel of the datapad

and slid the nail of his thumb between the battery and connector. He kept it there for just a second. There was a beep as the power reset.

Something else that most people didn't know was that if you triggered a reset on this model of datapad, which was Fleet issued, it would deactivate the biometric security until the user properly restarted the device.

Of course, with the biometric security deactivated, the device was still locked under the passcode. But Zemble was willing to bet that Fizza hadn't bothered to change the factory security code.

And when he flipped the datapad back over and tapped in the factory security code, every single one of Fizza's personal journal entries were immediately available for him to read.

He didn't bother with any of the older entries. What he needed, whatever it was, it was going to be more recent. Zemble scrolled through until he reached entries dated for around the time Cavige claimed to have met Fizza.

The first few contained nothing of note.

Then he came across the first mention of Cavige over two months ago:

I FINALLY AGREED to meet with Cavige. Mostly to get him to stop bothering me, I think. I don't know. Honestly, it all sounds a little crazy to me. I try not to judge other people's beliefs. Whatever helps them get through the night. But this...I don't know. It just seems to be a little crazy

THE NEXT ENTRY that mentioned Cavige was dated just a few days later.

. . .

I THOUGHT CAVIGE WAS CRAZY. *The things he was saying? Ancient immortal spirits causing all this...what did he call it? Phetans. It sounded* **crazy**.

But I'm not so sure anymore.

I'm starting to notice things. Things that don't seem quite right around me.

People looking at me differently.

People treating me differently.

Things are starting to smell, too.

I'm starting to wonder if I'm going a little crazy now.

A COUPLE OF WEEKS LATER:

WE'RE MAKING PROGRESS! *Cavige thinks most of phetans have been purged from me. Although, he's worried about my proximity to Reynoso. He believes that the ambassador is even more infected than I was. He's concerned that by maintaining my closeness to Reynoso I could become reinfected. What am I supposed to do? Quit my job? I can't do that. I'm on track to transfer out in less than a year. If I quit, what do I do? I'm back at ground zero. I'd be starting over from scratch. Cavige asks what's more important to me: my life or my career?*

THE NEXT DAY:

I HAD AN IDEA. *Cavige isn't totally on board with it. I don't know why. It's kind of brilliant, really.*

I feel amazing. My head is clear for the first time in months. The rashes are completely gone and I'm talking to my parents again since, hell, I don't know. I think the last time I spoke to either of them was before I left Earth and that was almost five years ago.

Obviously, this could help Ambassador Reynoso. I don't think there's anyone who could benefit from this more than the ambassador, especially if what Cavige says is true.

So why try to distance myself from the ambassador? I should bring him to the Church!

The alcohol, the prostitutes, the gambling, this could be huge for Ambassador Reynoso.

Cavige, though, he's hesitant. He keeps saying that the ambassador seems closed off and it might be too difficult to get through to him.

But if we don't try then what is the point of any this?

IT WAS another few weeks before Cavige came up again:

IT'S BEEN impossible to get the ambassador to even consider visiting the church. Cavige suggested we may have to get creative.

TWO WEEKS LATER FIZZA WROTE:

I'M NOT FEELING GREAT.
My head hurts.

. . .

ZEMBLE SKIPPED AHEAD to entries that were made just a week prior to Reynoso's death.

I'M NOT sure of anything anymore.
Cavige says it's okay. He says that it's normal. He says that the confusion, the missing nights, those are the effects of the phetans fighting back.
But I don't know anymore.
I think...

AFTER THAT, the entries became fewer and farther between. They hardly even counted as proper entries. Some were barely even a complete sentence. Most of it read like gibberish.

CAVIGE WANTED to talk about Reynoso again. I tried to stay focused this time. I tried to remember everything he wanted to talk about, but it kept slipping through me.
I don't think I'm well.
I don't know if I was ever well.

THEN HE REACHED the entry made the night before Reynoso died:

I'M afraid there's something broken in me.
I'm afraid I might do something terrible.

. . .

AFTER THAT, there was one more entry the morning of
Fizza's death:

I'M SORRY.

ZEMBLE SPENT another few minutes scrolling through the
other entries, skimming some, rereading others.

A few more pieces clicked into place.

Out of context, these were the ramblings of a madman.

But Zemble had context.

He looked at the leather-bound book on the nightstand.

He replayed the conversation with Cavige.

And then he focused on the sentence in Fizza's journal:

CAVIGE SUGGESTED we may have to get creative.

25

"KATHRYN STRAUB. It's been too long and not long enough."

Like most Chirotians, Viv'an Bendare had dark, purple skin. Unlike most Chirotians, however, her skin had a shimmer to it; a vague, sparkling, almost incandescent glow. When she stood still, it was a shimmering halo outlining her body. When she moved, it was like she left a little part of her behind; a sparkling, shimmering echo that matched her outline exactly.

And what an outline it was.

When Keane had seen her picture his first thought was that she was attractive. He couldn't help himself. It was an immediate reaction. A natural reaction. There wasn't anything necessarily lascivious about it. His mind simply acknowledged that she was an attractive woman.

In person, however, he had a completely different response.

His pulse quickened.

His hands felt clammy.

He felt blood rushing to other parts of his body that shouldn't have blood being rushed to at a moment like this.

Bendare's body was all curves and as Straub had already mentioned, the attractive crime lord was rather opposed to wearing outfits that covered too much of her body.

And what a body it was.

The silk robe, if you could even call it a robe, it was more of a singular stretch of satin that wrapped around her ample bosom and then just seemed to drop directly between her legs. And that was it. The rest of her shimmering body was exposed and Keane got the distinct impression that if a breeze were to suddenly sweep through the room, that single stretch of statin would simply slip away from her body with a relieving sigh.

Keane swallowed nervously and worked to keep his gaze locked on her eyes.

Then Bendare got up from her seat and walked over to them.

Her hips sashayed with every step, moving in time with the beat of his racing pulse. With every step, Keane's breath caught a little as he wondered if this was going to be the step that caused her simple outfit to drop from her body.

Bendare smiled as she approached them. It was like being smiled at by a viper and a shiver ran down Keane's spine.

"You brought a new friend," she said, making no effort to disguise the way her eyes roamed across Keane's body. "And I must say, I think I'm going to prefer Commander Keane over that boorish Leyla Lin."

She stepped up to him. They were so close Keane could feel her breath on his face. It smelled intoxicatingly sweet. There was a deep, primal instinct within him that screamed for him to grab her and pull her so close to him that their bodies would inevitably merge into one.

But then, remarkably, Keane remembered Rule Number One and he took one difficult step back.

Keane cleared his throat, coughing into his hand as he struggled to find something else to focus on other than Bendare.

Bendare's dark, pointed eyebrows went up. "Oh, well, somebody was paying attention." She turned to Straub. "I like him. You should have him transferred over."

"I'm not here to discuss my staffing procedures," Straub said, her arms folded as she affected a pose that projected the most irritated frustration she could manage.

Bendare laughed as though Straub had simply shared the most delightful risqué joke. She turned back to Keane, studying him a little more closely, letting her focus linger on his limbs that had been torn from his body by the Unity and then inexplicably restored by an entity from a higher dimension. "You look absolutely *remarkable* for a man who was nearly *dead*." She pressed her lips together, as though savoring the taste of something. "Actually, you look positively *delicious* for a man who, as I understand it, was considerably less than whole a mere few weeks ago."

Keane swallowed nervously again. He blinked and focused his eyes on her eyes, not that it seemed to make anything easier. Her eyes were like silver pools of light with incandescent blue pupils dancing around in them, threatening to pull him in, inch by inch. "My secret is that I try to make sure I eat all my vegetables and take all my vitamins."

Bendare laughed again and Keane nearly melted right there. "I like you." She looked at Straub. "I like him a lot."

"You want him?" Straub asked.

Keane jerked his head to face Straub. "Say what now?"

Straub glared at him. "Maybe get your tongue back in your mouth, Commander."

Keane's face turned bright red.

"Oh, please," Bendare said. "You shouldn't be so hard on him. After all, is it really his fault? You could have brought Leyla."

"Leyla would have broken your rules," Straub said.

"Yes, I suppose she would have," Bendare agree, looking at Keane with eyes that were almost laughing. "I guess we're all in agreement then: Commander Keane is the absolute best man for the job."

"I..." Keane started and then trailed off.

"It's okay," Bendare said, lowering her voice to a whisper. She took a step forward until their noses were almost touching. "I feel the same way. Don't think too deeply about it. Just go with it."

Keane let out a stuttering breath and nearly passed out from lightheadedness.

Abruptly, Bendare pivoted on her heel, turning in a circle as she looked for her faithful Vulderran assistant. "Jacoby?"

"Yes, ma'am?" Jacoby stepped forward into the room from the lift.

"Have you offered our guests any refreshments?"

"I'm afraid I have not. My apologies."

She sighed and waved her hand dismissively as she walked back to her seat.

"Would either of you care for some Bethari sparkling water?" Jacoby asked.

"No," Straub replied.

Keane coughed again, his throat very dry now, and raised his hand. "Actually I wouldn't say no to a glass."

Jacoby nodded and disappeared through another door off to their left.

At this point, there was simply no sense of scale

anymore on the *Soul of Obsession*. To Keane, everything felt too large to possibly be on the same ship.

The room that Bendare kept as her office, her meeting space, was a large, oval with a domed ceiling that was easily thirty feet above them. At the top of it was a clear glass enclosure, giving them a perfect view of the empty space outside. It was almost unnoticeable, though, in the whiteness of the room. The floors, the walls, and the furniture were all a brilliant shade of white that made it impossible to tell where the light in the room even emanated from.

The lift exit sat on the straight wall, almost thirty feet wide. It connected to a curved wall that took over the rest of the room. Coupled with the domed ceiling and the view of space, the design elements created an illusion that the room was even bigger than it actually was.

Bendare dropped herself onto a large chair with thick cushions. She let her leg drape over one of the armrests and, again the stretch of satin between her legs threatened to fall to the side completely. She gestured to the empty chairs adjacent to her own. "Please, have a seat."

Straub didn't move and so, subsequently, neither did Keane.

Bendare sighed theatrically. "So, Kathryn Straub, what brings you to my doorstep, after going through so much trouble to get me kicked off yours?"

Straub gestured with her hand indicating the surroundings and the ship as a whole. 'Feels like somebody's overcompensating."

"Hardly," Bendare replied. "If we're being honest, I should probably thank you for having me unceremoniously removed from your station. My accommodations since then have been quite the upgrade."

"Living your life to the fullest," Straub said with a hint of irony.

Bendare smiled coolly at her. "Why are you here, Kathryn. Because it's clearly not to take cheap shots at me and it is most definitely not to take advantage of my hospitality."

Straub scoffed at the mention of Bendare's hospitality.

Jacoby reappeared with a black tray and a single glass of Bethari sparkling water on it. He held it out to Keane.

Keane reached for the glass and then hesitated for a moment.

"Dear, you needn't worry," Bendare said sweetly. "I don't believe in poisoning people. It's a coward's way to deal with a problem."

"It's not you I'm worried about right now," Keane replied and glanced at Straub.

Bendare laughed again.

"Drink the water or don't," Straub said. "I don't really care one way or another."

"Sure," Keane muttered under his breath as he picked up the glass.

"Well?" Bendare prompted. "Are we going to get to the point or perhaps you'd like a little more foreplay, Kathryn?"

Keane nearly choked on his water. He wiped the back of his hand across his mouth as he looked back and forth between the two women. A playful smile danced across Bendare's face as Straub glared at her with all the intensity of a sun going supernova.

Straub folded her arms. "Ambassador Reynoso is dead."

Bendare's leg slid off the armrest as she straightened up in her seat, her playful attitude fading away. "What? What do you mean?"

"I mean exactly what I said," Straub replied. "Reynoso's dead."

Bendare didn't say anything. There was a numb expression settling in on her face.

Straub and Keane looked at each other. This wasn't the reaction they had been expecting.

Finally, Bendare leaned forward, folding her hands together and resting her elbows on the back of her legs. "What happened?"

Now it was Straub's turn not to say anything for a minute. She chose her words carefully. "That's a complicated answer."

"How so?"

"It's an open investigation."

Bendare looked back and forth between them. "He was murdered?"

Again, Straub didn't say anything.

Something clicked in Bendare's mind and she sat back. "You think I had something to do with it. *That's* why you're here."

"Your history with the ambassador," Straub started to say.

Bendare cut her off with a wave of her hand. "My history with Caldwell was hardly violent." The shock of the news was wearing off and Bendare was quickly finding herself back on familiar ground.

"Just because you didn't have a violent history, doesn't mean you wouldn't kill him," Straub said, although she was feeling less convinced of this theory by the minute.

Bendare carefully crossed her legs. "That may be true, Kathryn. But I was rather fond of Caldwell. Yes, he was an uncultured, alcoholic oaf." She smiled wanly at the memory.

"But he had a certain charm that I found made it easy to forgive him. Perhaps even too easy."

Straub and Keane exchanged looks with one other again.

"There's obviously more to this story," Bendare said. "Do please share. After all, you've gone through all this trouble, you might as well put in the effort of a good show."

Straub nodded at Keane. He finished the water and looked around for a place to set it down. When he couldn't find a convenient place, he simply lowered it to his side. "When was the last time you spoke with the ambassador?"

Bendare clapped. "Ah. So we're doing the full show. Alright. Let's do it then. This should be *fun*."

"We're not here to play a game," Straub said, her voice sounded short.

"But you're here on my time and I feel like playing," Bendare replied. "So you really don't have a say beyond that." She pressed the tips of her folded fingers to her lips for a moment as she ran through her memory. "Let's see. The last time I spoke to Caldwell. Well, that's a tricky question, isn't it?"

"Not really," Straub replied through gritted teeth.

Bendare smiled from behind her fingers. "Oh, please. We're all professionals here. We all know how this works. *I* know how this works. You don't ask a question unless you already know the answer. Or, at least what you believe the answer to be. So the real question is: What do you think you know?" She looked back and forth between them, tapping her fingers against her lips. "My last communication with Caldwell was weeks ago. He had reached out to me about obtaining a supply of Chirot graded opium."

Straub winced at the mention of the illegal drug.

Bendare laughed again, clearly enjoying the discomfort she was causing Straub. "Obviously I wasn't able to assist him as I'm not in the business of trafficking illegal, mind altering substances." She uncrossed her legs and then slowly crossed them again, draping her arms along the armrests of her chair. "Now, I've shown you mine. Why don't you show me yours?"

"That's not the communication we have," Straub said.

"Of course it isn't," Bendare replied, sounding unsurprised.

"According to our sources, you contacted Reynoso within the last forty-eight hours," Straub said.

"Oh, did I?" Bendare raised a bemused eyebrow. "And what did I say in this alleged message?"

Straub shifted her weight, growing more uncomfortable with the situation by the moment. "You wanted to have a meeting with Reynoso in person, on V Deck, last night."

"I did? And did I happen to mention why I wanted to meet with Caldwell on V Deck?" Bendare asked.

Straub took a breath.

"Don't give up now, Kathryn," Bendare said. "Go for the punchline. I'm sure we're both going to absolutely laugh our heads off."

Straub pressed her lips together so tightly they formed a single line. "How do I know you're not lying?"

"You don't," Bendare said. "But to be fair, I've never actually lied to you before. So one would hope that our history together would buy me a little consideration."

"According to the message," Straub said. "You were attempting to blackmail Reynoso about a drug deal he was orchestrating with surviving members of the Veneer government."

Bendare wiggled her fingers excitedly. "Oooh, that does sound *juicy*."

"And you want us to believe that you didn't send that message?" Straub said.

"I want a great many things, Kathryn," Bendare said. "What you believe isn't among them. The facts are simply the facts. Whether you believe them or not, it doesn't really matter to me." She held up one finger. "First off, you have no legal authority here on this vessel. Second, I have no intention of violating the ban you placed on me in regards to the *Atlantic*. Third, no I did not send that message. Fourth, Caldwell orchestrating anything outside of his gentlemanly parts sounds a bit far-fetched, doesn't it?" She pressed her hands together and then spread them apart. "But I'm sure all this has occurred to you. As has the fact that you have no record of me stepping foot into your little fiefdom since you removed me from it months ago. So, one wonders, why are you really here? What did you really expect to get from this?"

"You've been here for two weeks," Straub said. "You really expect me to believe you haven't stepped foot off this ship?"

"Well, what do your station records say?"

"Records can be faked," Straub said. "Hacked. Deleted."

Bendare raised her eyebrows again. "And do you really think I would go through all that trouble? After all, I could simply pay someone to kill Caldwell for me and I would never have to leave the comfort of my own home."

"But you don't like poison," Keane said.

Bendare turned to him. Again, her playful attitude started to slip away. "Is that what happened?"

"It's an ongoing investigation," Straub said.

"And you can't tell me the cause of death because then you can't catch me lying when I reveal that I knew the cause all along." Bendare shook her head slowly. "Mr. Jacoby."

The Vuldeeran stepped forward. "Yes, ma'am."

"I believe Kathryn here is going to ask for an alibi. I would like to supply her with that information before she feels the need to ask."

Jacoby paused. "Are you sure about that?"

Bendare picked at something on her satin wrap. "Yes."

Jacoby nodded and produced a datapad from his coat. After a few taps, he looked up and addressed Straub. "Per Ms. Bendare's orders, I have forwarded you her alibi for last night. Obviously, we do not know when the ambassador expired, but that's not particularly relevant given the content of the information provided. As you will see, Ms. Bendare was otherwise occupied for the entirety of the evening."

"And as she already pointed out, she could have paid someone to do it," Keane said.

"Yes, well, if Ms. Bendare doesn't mind me speaking for her, in this particular instance, the burden of guilt is on you to prove," Jacoby replied. "Ms. Bendare isn't required to prove that she did not contact an unknown person who you have no particular lead on and acquire their alleged services to allegedly murder Ambassador Reynoso."

Straub just shook her head. "And what's this alibi you feel so confident it?"

Jacoby shifted uncomfortably. "I'd rather not say, due to its sensitive nature."

Bendare laughed softly. "That's why I love you, Mr. Jacoby." She locked eyes with Straub. "The file that my associate forwarded to you, Kathryn, is a media file approximately six hours in length, in which I was engaged with multiple other individuals, who will all testify to my presence there. Not that it should be in question, since you'll be able to clearly denote my uninterrupted presence from the file." She smiled lasciviously. "I should warn you; you may want a very, very, very cold shower after watching it."

26

According to the *Atlantic's* records, Joseph Michael Cavige arrived sixteen months ago.

Zemble didn't know why he wanted to know this. After leaving Fizza's quarters, he went to the *Atlantic's* security offices and settled into an empty console where he could work uninterrupted. Again, he wasn't entirely certain what he was looking for. He had a vague notion of something, but no hard evidence to back it up. But what would constitute as hard evidence in this case? Would he be so lucky to find the proverbial smoking gun? He didn't think so. Cavige wasn't sloppy.

Zemble skimmed through the *Atlantic's* records on Cavige, again, looking for anything that would jump out at him.

Cavige had made the trip from Earth on a private transport ship called *Fortune's Glory*. He arrived with six other members of the Church of Eternal Clarity. They were each granted a conditional visa that had been upgraded to permanent resident status after six weeks. Standard protocol for most individuals relocating from Earth.

The Church of Eternal Clarity was opened six days after Cavige gained permanent residence status. Zemble made note of that.

Like most organizations on the station, the *Atlantic* didn't keep any detailed records on the church itself. It made note of its tax status, operational hours and staff. It was a short entry.

Zemble moved to the local news on the *Atlantic*. They had a little more on the church, but not much.

There was a brief article on the Church of Eternal Clarity's growth. It went from the six members to over nearly a hundred within its first two months. Zemble made a note of this, too.

He found a small article in the social section that made mention of a fundraiser that had been attended by prominent residents of the *Atlantic*. Pictured standing together were Cavige and Pastor Loring. The article was dated nearly a year ago. By Zemble's count, that was at least two lies he had caught Cavige in.

There was no data available on any of the members of the church outside of the six that arrived with Cavige and even their entries were sparse. Membership within the Church of Eternal Clarity was apparently an extremely private matter.

Zemble came across one article that spoke, tangentially, of one member of the church: Captain Maddock of the *Tomahawk*. Zemble made a note of this, too.

The UPA had no regulations against religious affiliations among its members. In general, though, the Fleet frowned upon its people being associated with cult-like organizations.

Something about Captain Maddock bugged at Zemble and he switched the parameters of his search.

There was plenty of information available to him on Captain Maddock. He had been promoted from first officer of the *Lexington* two years ago. The *Tomahawk* was his second command after a brief stint in charge of a small medical ship, the *Blackwell*. He had multiple commendations and awards. According to various notes in his file, Zemble surmised he was on the fast track to admiralty.

Another quick search revealed that there were no currently serving admirals that had any known connections to the Church of Eternal Clarity. Although, Admiral Mccall, retired six years ago, was rumored to have been a member.

Mccall was currently deceased. He passed away after his retirement due to complications from Nirmal lung cancer.

Zemble widened the scope of his search beyond the *Atlantic*.

He found over a hundred or so pieces pertaining to Cavige on the intergalactic newsfeeds. Most of them related to his philanthropical work. Zemble read the first few articles in their entirety and then after that he started skimming them. He was looking for something to pop at him. What, though, he wasn't certain. They read like puff pieces, or worse, press releases directly from the Church of Eternal Clarity. There were a handful of more obscure articles that focused on the more suspect nature of the church and Cavige's questionable role in it. These articles didn't contain anything that he hadn't already read, though.

Every article had the same basic template of information: Despite his youthful appearance Cavige was sixty-two years old, having been born on Earth in a small town in Pennsylvania. He had been a member of the Church of Eternal Clarity since he was a teenager, after having been introduced to it by his father, Phillip Cavige. Cavige suffered from asthma and intense allergies. Allegedly, after his first assay session, Cavige was cured of both the asthma and the allergies, according to him and his father. This convinced the family to join the Church of Eternal Clarity full-time. Phillip Cavige uprooted his wife, his eldest son and the twins to Modesto, California where the church's headquarters were at the time.

Cavige had two siblings. His older brother, Phillip Cavige Jr, served as an accountant for the church for about thirteen years before leaving. Some of the more obscure articles, articles that, according to the search algorithms, the church had made a concerted effort to suppress, mentioned that after Phillip Cavige Jr. left the church he was completely excommunicated and cut off from all contact from the Cavige family. According to the church, he had led a misinformation campaign for many years in an attempt to discredit the church. He passed away a few years before, penniless, as the Church of Eternal Clarity spent nearly the rest of his adult life suing him for every slanderous thing he said about them. Zemble could only find one quote where Cavige discussed his brother. It was from an article covering Phillip Cavige Jr.'s death: "I understand that for a select few, this is a sad day. But for me, I lost my brother many years ago. Today is simply the day we bury the corpse of a man who did not realize he was already dead."

Joseph Michael Cavige's other sibling was his twin sister, Johanna Michelle Cavige. She was mentioned even less. After the first few articles, she disappeared almost completely. What few references Zemble could find were vague and just addressed her as "Cavige's twin sister who held a lower executive position within the church." Zemble couldn't find any explanation of what this position was.

Cavige's twin sister was simply a footnote in his history. This bothered Zemble. Again, he couldn't put his finger on why. But that voice at the back of his head poked at him about her.

So Zemble found himself shifting his search to Johanna Michelle Cavige.

At first, he just found the same articles about her brother. So he started over from scratch.

Again, he found nothing new.

That thing nagged at him again.

Johanna Michelle Cavige.

Zemble stared at the screen, waiting for something to jump out at him.

Johanna Michelle Cavige.

What did it matter? She wasn't here. He wanted her brother anyway.

Johanna Michelle *Cavige*.

It finally clicked. The little voice at the back of his head spoke up a little louder.

Cavige.

That was her maiden name. He couldn't find anything about her because she had married and changed her name?

This made sense to Zemble, but he still didn't see any connection.

He went back farther in his search, focusing on the local government records in California. He got lucky fifteen minutes later when he found a marriage license under the name of Johanna Michelle Cavige and Monroe Hansma. After that, he started to find a lot more.

Johanna Cavige Hansma resigned from her position within the church after her husband was appointed Earth's Ambassador to the Haka. Nothing suggested that she left the church. So she was, presumably still in good standing with the Church of Eternal Clarity.

Again, Zemble wasn't certain why he cared.

Cavige's brother seemed like a more interesting lead to follow. Something to use as evidence against the church's more questionable extra-legal antics.

And then he stumbled across an obituary notice for Johanna Hansma. The article was from thirty years ago. She passed away from an apparent suicide, having hanged herself.

That voice at the back of Zemble's head poked at him again. He made a dismissive wave with his hand; totally unaware he was doing it.

He stopped skimming and started reading the article from the beginning.

She had been found by her husband, Ambassador Hansma, after struggling with a bout of depression for several months. She left no note or any explanation as to why she might have killed herself.

At some point, Zemble stopped reading and instead focused on the second photo attached to the article. It was a somber moment of Ambassador Hansma as he watched his wife lowered into the ground. But all Zemble could see was the younger man standing just off to the side, near the background of the group. It was possible that if Zemble had not been in the middle of this particular investigation, he would not have even noticed the man. Thirty years ago, the man was a dashingly handsome individual. He had a strong jawline, a flat stomach, a full head of dark hair and charismatic eyes that had yet to be dulled by years of constant alcohol. He was nearly unrecognizable.

It was Caldwell Reynoso.

27

"COMMANDER? A moment of your time, please, if you don't mind."

Jacoby caught Keane just before he stepped onto the lift, but after Straub had already got on. In the time it took for Jacoby to call for Keane, the doors slid shut and Straub was whisked away.

"Somehow I'm definitely going to get in trouble for this," Keane muttered under his breath. He turned to face the approaching Vulderran. The disembarking ramp shook slightly under Jacoby's feet as he descended from gate 16. "What can I do for you, Mr. Jacoby? Please tell me there's not another orgy Bendare wants me to view."

Jacoby grimaced. "My apologies. Ms. Bendare tends to have issues with…boundaries."

"Sure. Boundaries. We'll call it that."

"She means well," Jacoby said.

"Please tell me you didn't stop me so I could listen to your excuses for her bizarre behavior. Because, I have to tell you, you are the first Vulderran I've met and I'm thoroughly underwhelmed," Keane said. "The chief engineer of the *Defiance* is constantly uttering Vulderran curses and it's never the same one twice. The stories he's told me...do not match the man standing before me right now."

Jacoby adjusted his outfit with an obvious sense of pride. "I will take that as a compliment. Thank you."

"Take it however you want," Keane said.

"My people do have a tendency to lean into their profane habits a little more than others," Jacoby said with a distasteful expression. "But I assure you, I am not here to apologize for anything Ms. Bendare has said or done."

"Then why are you here?" Keane asked.

"It's come to our attention that your investigation is currently following another lead at this time," Jacoby said. "A rather promising lead, as it were."

Keane set his jaw and folded his arms. "And how exactly did this come to your attention in the short time it took us to leave your ship?"

"Ms. Bendare is not without her means."

"Which means *what* exactly?"

"Unfortunately I am not at liberty to divulge those means," Jacoby said apologetically.

Keane shook his head. "I'm not going to comment on other potential leads in an investigation where your boss is a person of interest."

Jacoby waved a dismissive hand. "Please. We both know that Ms. Bendare is nothing of the sort at this point. Joseph Michael Cavige, however-"

Keane held up a hand, cutting him off. "How the hell did you even get that name?"

"As I already explained, I am not at liberty to say."

"What about when I haul you in for questioning?"

"Even then," Jacoby said.

"You're interfering with an ongoing murder investigation."

"This hardly counts as interference, Commander," Jacoby said, a pained expression on his face. "I'm simply here to pass along information of note."

Keane's face settled into a scowl. "Information of *note*."

Jacoby seemed unperturbed by Keane's attitude. "In addition to Ms. Bendare's now unnecessary alibi, I've forwarded along a list of individuals you may want with speak to in regards to Mr. Cavige's whereabouts over the last twenty-four hours. We believe these individuals may help you in establishing a timeline of events for Mr. Cavige."

"I can't take this," Keane said.

Jacoby nodded. "I understand, of course. Ms. Bendare would like me to assure you that she does not need nor want any form of compensation for this information."

"That is *not* what I was thinking about at all," Keane said. "This information is *tainted*."

Jacoby frowned. "Because of where's coming from?"

"Exactly."

"Ms. Bendare has no ulterior motives for passing along this information," Jacoby said.

"She doesn't need ulterior motives," Keane said. "Her history-Her *alleged* history will taint it."

"Well, I'm afraid then I don't know what to tell you, Commander. You are, of course, free not to use this information," Jacoby said. "But the simple fact of the matter is that Ms. Bendare is nothing more than a concerned citizen, and a hurting friend, who simply wants justice for Ambassador Reynoso."

"Justice," Keane echoed, his voice sounding hollow.

"The truth comes in all sorts of flavors, Commander," Jacoby said. "That reminds me. Ms. Bendare also wanted me to inform you that her organization will be providing inter-ference with the Church of Eternal Clarity's lawyers. They can be a nasty bunch to deal with and Ms. Bendare wanted to make sure you have the time necessary to build your case and access whatever you may need, not only from Mr. Cavige's private database, but also the church's."

"You can't do that."

"Of course we can," Jacoby said. "We are free citizens operating within the legal bounds of the UPA. However our actions may positively affect your investigation is merely a fortunate side effect."

"That's not..." Keane trailed off, unsure of what to say.

Jacoby grinned and tipped his hat. "It was a pleasure meeting you. I look forward to our next conversation."

"Our *next* conversation?"

Jacoby headed back to the ship. "Ms. Bendare finds you to be a fascinating individual. And in my experience, when Ms. Bendare finds you to be fascinating that's the beginning of a very long and fruitful relationship. Have a good day, Commander."

Jacoby disappeared back through the airlock.

Keane hit the call button for the lift as he pulled out his communicator and dialed up Zemble's number.

28

"WHAT WOULD you say if I told you your god was a lie, Mr. Zemble?" Cavige seemed unsurprised to see Zemble as he entered the sanctuary of the Church of Eternal Clarity.

"I'd say you're pretty much on brand," Zemble replied.

Cavige laughed. It echoed loudly through the empty auditorium. He stood at his pulpit, elevated from the empty seats by a good six feet. The room had a vaulted ceiling and could easily seat a couple hundred people. Now, though, it was empty. Cavige and Zemble were the only two occupants, each standing on opposite sides of the room.

Behind Cavige on a black wall were two raised, golden interlinked triangles. The light of the sanctuary glinted off them and Zemble knew, somehow, the triangles weren't made from artificially manufactured material. They were genuine gold.

Cavige pressed his hands against the edges of his podium, eyeing Zemble as he made his way down the center aisle.

"I knew you were going to be here," Cavige said.

"Did you now," Zemble said. He didn't seem surprised or impressed by this.

Cavige nodded, sage-like. "I did. Just like I know how this is going to end."

Zemble stopped in the middle of the sanctuary. "And how exactly is it going to end?"

Cavige pulled his hands free and raised them to the ceiling. "With your eyes truly being opened." He smiled. "It was providential we met last night, you know."

Zemble grunted and resumed approaching the podium. Each footstep sounded like a dead weight echoing along the floor. "Yeah, I had been thinking the same thing."

"Oh?" Cavige leaned forward, resting his forearms on the podium.

"I found it suspect that you would approach me the night before I was assigned a murder investigation in which you would end up being a factor."

"A factor?" Cavige echoed.

"It's more polite than saying a person of interest," Zemble replied.

"And is that what I am? A person of interest?" Cavige drummed his fingers against the podium. "Interesting. You know, I find it rather interesting that we would cross paths like this as well."

"The Lord works in mysterious ways," Zemble said.

"Of course, of course," Cavige agreed. "Unless, of course, your god is nothing but a precious little lie you tell yourself every night so you can sleep without the horrors of your reality threatening to crush your subconscious."

Zemble made another grunting noise, although this time it sounded more like a half laugh.

Cavige smiled, as if he was in on the joke. "And what divine purpose are we being brought together for?"

"Justice."

"Just us?" Cavige said, with a cheeky grin. He raised his arms and twirled his hands with a slight flourish.

Zemble stopped just short of the stage. "You're under arrest."

Cavige flinched. It lasted less than a second and had Zemble not be so focused on him, he would have missed it. He slowly lowered his hands back to the pulpit, letting them rest casually on the surface. A bemused smile passed across his mouth. "And what am I being arrested for, Mr. Zemble?"

"The murders of Ambassador Caldwell Reynoso and Imaad Fizza."

Cavige tilted his head to the side, as if appearing to be thinking it over for a moment. "Curious. I must confess," he paused for a second and then continued, "This is news to me as I don't recall having killed either of those men."

"You recruited Fizza into your church and manipulated him into revealing any information you could use to kill Reynoso without it ever getting back to you." Zemble held up the book he had found in Fizza's quarters. "Your bible's written in a post-hypnotic code. It's how your church successfully brainwashes so many of its members. Every assay session they're encouraged to spend some time in the 'scriptures,' where everything you broke down in them is subtly reinforced." He tossed the book up on the stage. "These sorts of things don't regularly work on Elwats. Our brains produce a hormone that makes it difficult for us to be affected by subliminal messages. It's why there's no advertising network on my home planet. It's also why we tend not to fall prey to cults."

Cavige took a breath and slowly exhaled, tapping his fingers against the podium. "Mr. Zemble, I believe you are making a terrible mistake."

"I don't think so," he replied. "Through Fizza you gained access to Reynoso's medical records. Once you had those, you knew about the baalhanno parasites and from there, I'm sure you were willing to put in a little research to determine exactly what kind of damage could be done with those little parasites. Once you settled on your method, you used Fizza to create the fake Veneer drug deal and the blackmail message to point to Bendare. But you knew none of that would hold up, so then you killed Fizza and made it look like a suicide, knowing that once we learned Bendare was a dead end we'd double back to Fizza and assume he was the one behind the fake Veneer drug deal. From there, it would stand to reason Reynoso caught on to the Veneer deal that Fizza was orchestrating and he threatened to expose Fizza. Feeling threatened, Fizza killed Reynoso and then took his own life out of guilt."

Cavige stopped tapping his fingers. He looked at Zemble with a raised eyebrow of curiosity. "And why would I bother going through all this trouble, Mr. Zemble. Because it does sound like quite a bit of trouble."

"Because a little over thirty years ago when Reynoso was an aide to Ambassador Monroe Hansma he had an affair with Hansma's wife, your twin sister. Shortly after the affair ended, she committed suicide in a manner not unlike Fizza's death." Zemble pointed at Cavige. "You held Reynoso responsible for that."

Cavige's face darkened. "My dear sister's death was over three decades ago, Mr. Zemble. Not only do I not appreciate you dragging her name through the mud like this, why the hell would I wait so damn long for such a petty thing as *revenge*?"

Zemble shrugged. "Maybe because you didn't know for certain. Maybe because you didn't have the resources then that you have now. Or maybe it's simply because it took you this long to work up the nerve. It's not easy to kill a man. I know from personal experience."

"That sounds like a threat, Mr. Zemble," Cavige said.

"Then I would suggest you request Doctor Hogle to examine your hearing after your arraignment," Zemble replied.

Cavige didn't say anything for a moment. He just stood there, his hands resting on the edges of his podium as he studied Zemble. "Tell me, Commander, how did you exactly come to these conclusions? How did you reach this particular endpoint? What was it that led you down this path?"

Zemble started walking again, moving for the stairs at the edge of the stage. "That's a good question and I don't know if I have a good answer for you."

"That's not the sort of explanation that's going to hold up in a court of law," Cavige pointed out.

"No, that's true," Zemble agreed. "But I've got enough of a paper trail that I think a judge and, more importantly, a jury will find you guilty. Fizza kept a journal. A private journal you probably didn't even know about. It's a pretty clear map of a man losing his mind after coming into contact with you. Your sister's marriage and Reynoso's position thirty years ago are all a matter of public record."

"But whether or not they had an affair hardly is," Cavige said. He pulled back slightly as Zemble stepped onto the stage.

Zemble nodded. "Except that Reynoso's a noted philanderer and in his biography, Ambassador Hansma made several remarks about his first wife, your sister, engaging in an extramarital affair before her passing. He doesn't name who she might have been cheating on him with. But I don't think it's a stretch to get a jury to believe that it was Reynoso.

Especially considering that shortly before her death Hansma had Reynoso abruptly transferred out of his office."

Cavige twitched again. Now standing directly in front of him, Zemble could see a cold sweat had broken out across Cavige's face.

"Your Lord works in mysterious ways, eh?" Cavige said.

"I've been thinking the very same thing," Zemble replied.

"Is that what you're going to say when you get called to testify?" Cavige asked. "Because that sort of thing could cast doubts, you know."

Zemble nodded. "I'll worry about that when I get to it. But I think it's safe to say that if God brought me this far, He's got a plan to carry it over the finish line."

Cavige frowned. "I have to admit, Mr. Zemble, I'm disappointed in you."

"I can live with that."

"I thought you a kindred spirit," Cavige continued.

"Then you're a terrible judge of character."

"I thought you were smarter than this," Cavige said.

Zemble shrugged. "That's the problem with expectations. Look at it from my point of view," Zemble said. "Everybody expected this was going to have some kind of far-reaching implications. That Reynoso's death was going to set off some kind of altercation with the Veneer. Instead, it was just *this*. A petty little revenge story."

The twitch turned into a tremble and Cavige gripped the podium tighter to keep from trembling out of control. "I know what you're trying to do."

Zemble loomed over him. He folded his arms. "And what's that?"

"You're trying to trick me into confessing."

"Trick you," Zemble echoed.

"It won't work."

"Okay."

"Because it's not true."

"Uh-huh."

"You don't have any authority to even be here right now," Cavige said, his voice sounding slightly more frantic.

"I absolutely do," Zemble said and gestured back to the front doors.

Cavige turned and saw that four other *Atlantic* security officers had entered. Each one was armed.

"It's circumstantial at best," Cavige said, his voice was getting lower.

"I have three people willing to testify under oath that they saw you down on V Deck," Zemble said. "Now, I don't think you killed Reynoso when you were down there. That already happened when you had Fizza start to poison him earlier in the week. But I can put you down there, within fifteen or twenty feet of where we found Reynoso's body. I'd like to see you explain what you were doing down there."

Cavige didn't say anything, he just stared at the four security officers.

"I also have a witness who can place you leaving Fizza's quarters within the window of his death," Zemble said. "And, yes, while you were smart enough to have Fizza purchase the synthehol, it's your search history that's filled with info regarding the baalharno parasites. So, sure, you could argue it's all circumstantial, but I'm feeling pretty good about our odds here."

Cavige jerked back around and pointed at Zemble. His face was nearly as red as Zemble's skin. "If you do this, we will *destroy* you in ways that you cannot possibly begin to imagine," he snarled. "Death will be a sweet release for you. Your life will simply become one unending source of pain and frustration and the only possible way to escape it will be *death*."

Zemble grunted and nodded his head, as if Cavige had described nothing more controversial than Dreks' upcoming menu changes. "Maybe." He took a long pause. "But I recently had the misfortune to spend some time in another dimension where I was inundated with pain. Endless physical pain that permeated every inch of my being. I couldn't tell you how long I was there or how long the pain lasted. All I know is that it became such an endless constant for me that now, to this very day, I find myself missing that pain like you might miss a limb." Zemble reached out and placed a heavy hand on Cavige's shoulder. Instinctively, Cavige tried to jerk out of his grip, but Zemble's hand was firm and Cavige was only going to move if Zemble wanted him to. "So I think I'll be able to handle anything your so-called church can throw at me. The real question is whether or not you can handle prison time."

Cavige looked at the large hand sitting on his shoulder. He said nothing. He did nothing.

And then, he started laughing.

"What's so funny?" Zemble asked.

Cavige didn't respond. His laughter just got louder as it transitioned from normal to hysterical. Tears formed at the corners of his eyes as he clutched his arms around his midsection. Cavige dropped to his knees, the laughter had clearly become uncontrollable.

Zemble gestured for the security officers to approach.

Cavige toppled over onto his side, curling up into the fetal position as he just kept laughing and laughing and laughing.

29

"WHAT ARE YOU READING?"

Nax looked up from the datapad in his lap. He sat naked in the center of his bed. "It's an obscure piece of work by Grugneod."

"Ah." Hawkins nodded, sitting down on the edge of the bed. She wore her Fleet uniform, although the front zipper was down to her navel and she wore nothing under it. "Noted Vulderran poet. Most of his material inspires depression, doesn't it?"

Nax shrugged his slender shoulders and turned back to the datapad. "There's nuance to it."

"Nuance?" Hawkins said. "You read me one of his poems once and I cried for nearly two hours."

"I believe that was the point," Nax replied.

"How is that the point?"

"Specifically?"

"Yes, *specifically*."

Nax looked up from the datapad. "I honestly don't know. Perhaps the next time I'm presented with the opportunity to travel back in time I will endeavor to reach out and find

Grugneod in hopes of starting a conversation with him about the meaning of his work."

Hawkins pouted. "Well, aren't you in a mood."

"I am not in a 'mood.'"

"I came here with good news," she said.

"What good news could you have possibly arrived with?"

Hawkins looked down at her outfit, idly tracing her finger along the open edge of her uniform. "I don't know if it's worth passing along now. Not with you being in a mood. You might take it the wrong way."

Nax wordlessly turned back to his book.

"Seriously?" Hawkins asked. "That's it?"

"Presumably you'll share with me whatever it is you want to share with me when you're ready to share it with me," he said, not bothering to look up this time.

She sighed. "Bon Dov."

"I'm sorry?" Nax looked up at her.

She leaned in, smiling. "Bon Dov."

"So you've mentioned."

"He's a Natuzzi from, oh, I don't know, two hundred years back who suffered from Fey's Euphoria. He was diagnosed as the youngest to ever contract it at the time." She curled up her legs unto the bed. "What? You're looking at me like I just suggested that you need to learn to start growing hair."

"I'm just curious to hear more," Nax said carefully.

"Okay. Well, despite his condition, he went on to live a rather productive life. He got married, a lovely woman by the name of J'll Tiss. She was a member of the Science Parliament. They had three children, none of whom ever showed any signs of Fey's. In fact, all three of them went on to marry and have children of their own. Dov had nearly a dozen grandchildren. Can you believe that?"

"I cannot," Nax replied truthfully.

"He even held down a lucrative career composing haunting nursery limericks," Hawkins continued. "Which, admittedly, is a bit on the nose for somebody who has a condition wherein it's difficult for him to discern between reality and fantasy. But, he made it work for him. Bon Dov had a long, full, fruitful and productive life. He even lived to a nice, ripe old age, one hundred and six, I believe."

Nax frowned.

Hawkins tilted her head, looking at him from an upside-down angle. "What? This is supposed to make you feel better. You're supposed to be encouraged. This doesn't have to be a death sentence. It doesn't have to be a bad thing. And, yet you're sitting there like I've just told you you've got thirty-six hours to live."

Nax turned off the datapad and got to his feet. "I appreciate the sentiment."

"You appreciate the sentiment?" she sat upright and watched as he slowly got dressed. "That's not exactly the reaction I was hoping for."

"What kind of reaction were you hoping for?"

"One that was going to be the opposite of you getting dressed." Hawkins gestured to her provocative outfit. "I didn't put this on because I thought I was going to do a shift on the bridge."

Nax zipped up his uniform. "Except that you don't have shifts anymore as you're dead."

She rolled her eyes. "Yes, I'm aware of that. You haven't forgotten, so naturally I haven't forgotten. I'm just being cheeky." She held out her hand, beckoning back to the bed. "Seriously, come back here."

"I can't."

"You *can't*?" Hawkins repeated. "Where are you going?"

Nax paused at the door. "I believe I'm going to find Warrick."

"As opposed to this?" Again, she gestured to the naked skin that was showing from underneath her uniform.

Nax closed his eyes and took a deep breath. He exhaled slowly. "Yes."

Hawkins folded her arms. "What's the problem here?"

He opened his eyes and looked at her. "The problem is that I've never heard of Bon Dov."

30

ABOVE THE ION DRIVE, something exploded.

"Westin, you gorram pile of Nunzotov dog shit!" Warrick shouted as plasma sparks rained down across engineering and everyone ducked for cover.

An alarm started to blare. It was so loud Warrick could feel the floor plating beneath him shake.

"Somebody shut off that frelling alarm!" Warrick snapped. "All the main power relays are still shut down, I don't know what the hell the damn thing is going on about." He wiped soot from his face. "And then somebody tell Westin to get her gorram ass away from the secondary propulsion drives before she blasts us and half the station into the nearest star." He muttered a handful of Vulderran curses as he looked around the small station on the second level of engineering and found Nax standing off to the side. "What the hell do you want?"

"To talk," Nax replied.

Warrick just grunted and turned back to the station. In his left hand he held an auto-sequencing wrench. He moved the wrench to his mouth and used both hands to pull out a wide cable from behind the station. Carefully he wedged the cable along the corner of the station and then dropped the auto-sequencing wrench into his now free right hand. He thumbed on the wrench and held it to the open port on the cable. A moment later the entire second level of engineering went dark.

Somebody yelped loudly as they banged into equipment they suddenly couldn't see.

"Was that supposed to happen?" Nax asked.

"No," Warrick grumbled. He fumbled in the dark for another few seconds, reaching back behind the station for a series of open fuses. A moment later, emergency lighting kicked on, casting the area in an eerie red glow. Warrick brushed his hands off and turned to Nax. "Okay, fine. You want to talk? You can have five minutes. That's how long it's going take to for the plasma breakers to reset."

Nax didn't say anything for a moment. Behind Warrick Hawkins appeared, her uniform zipped up in a more professional manner.

"You're wasting precious time here, Nax," Warrick said. "I've got a ship to put back together."

Hawkins peeked behind the station and made a disgusted face. "Is that what he says he's doing?"

"If you've got something to say, you better say it," Warrick said.

"Actually, I'm pretty curious about what you have to say, too," Hawkins said, leaning against the station.

Warrick glanced in the direction Nax was staring but obviously didn't see Hawkins.

Nax flicked his gaze back to Warrick. "I have a confession to make, Jaxson."

"Yeah? Are you the one going around tripping up all the gravity plating?"

"I'm seeing Grace," Nax said.

Hawkins smiled. "While I'm glad to see you taking my advice, I still feel like this is a conversation that didn't have to happen right *now*."

"I've been...hallucinating her since the *Eternal Hand of God*," Nax continued.

"Nax," Warrick began, but Nax cut him off with a raise of his hand.

"Much like you, at first I believed that I was suffering from some form of Fey's Euphoria."

"*Some* form of Fey's Euphoria?" Warrick said. "You're talking to a dead woman, Nax. A *dead woman*."

"Well," Hawkins said, "I may be dead, but that doesn't mean I'm still not a lively conversationalist, among other...*things*." She smiled and winked at Nax.

Nax struggled to stay focused on Warrick. "However, given my current condition, I didn't believe it was something that would cause any conflict with my role on the ship."

"You didn't believe..." Warrick stared at him in disbelief. "You're *hallucinating* your dead girlfriend. How the *hell* do you think that wouldn't cause *problems*?"

"In your defense, I have done my best to remain as professional as possible when you're on duty," Hawkins said.

Nax took a moment to steady his voice. "I have a firm grasp on what is and what is not real. I was aware that I was engaged in an affair with a figment of my imagination."

"Sounds like you're splitting Fim'ai ass hairs," Warrick said.

"One of the primary symptoms of Fey's Euphoria is the inability to discern between what is real and what is not. That is not my problem."

"That is very true," Hawkins agreed. "You haven't forgotten, for one moment, that I'm not real. You've certainly tried, though. You just haven't been able to give yourself over completely to the fantasy. I won't lie, though, it stings a little."

"That doesn't mean it isn't going to become a problem. Nobody with Fey's gets better, Nax. They just get *worse*. It's a degenerative disease."

"No one is more aware of that than I am," Nax said. "I am all too cognizant of the dangers that Fey's presents."

"Which is why you've been going around lying about it."

"It is a unique situation," Nax said. "I could not simply approach Dr. Rabkin as he wouldn't have any point of reference to assist me. This condition is not something off-worlders are permitted to be aware of. The fact that you are, is unique and privileged and I wish that you would appreciate that."

"I appreciate it just *fine*," Warrick said. "But my appreciation of it doesn't trump me being worried about my friend."

Nax inhaled through his nose. "Something else has happened that has also caused me to believe I am not suffering from Fey's."

"Oh? What exactly is that?" Warrick folded his arms.

Nax glanced at Hawkins again. She, too, was waiting with bated breath.

"Fey's Euphoria creates a break between reality and fantasy in the mind of its subject," Nax said. "But the fantasy is still drawn from the mind of the individual. The unreality can be built from memories and experiences the individual has actually experienced." He paused for a second. "Grace has...brought up information that I would not have known."

Warrick frowned. "What the hell does that mean?"

"Are you familiar with the name Bon Dov?"

Warrick thought about it for a moment and then shook his head. "No. Should I be?"

"Apparently he was one of the youngest Natuzzi to ever suffer from Fey's Euphoria."

"Huh. I didn't know that."

"Neither did I," Nax replied. He gave it a moment to sink in for Warrick. As understanding dawned Warrick's eyes widened. Nax nodded. "If this Grace Hawkins is a figment of my own diseased mind, how is she passing along new information to me?"

"That's a damn good question." Warrick said. "Do you have an answer?

Nax looked at Hawkins again. Her smile faltered and something in her eyes flickered in an unfamiliar way.

"No, I do not," Nax said. "No, I do not."

31

Leyla Lin answered her door to find Keane standing on the other side.

"What the hell is this?" Lin asked, arms folded. She was dressed out of uniform in a pair of gray sweatpants and an oversized matching shirt with a wide neck that hung off her shoulder.

Keane held up the bottle of Relese Rosso wine. "It's a peace offering."

Lin took the bottle and checked the vintage. "For what?"

"For stealing your case."

"Suddenly you outrank Commodore Straub?"

Keane paused, scratching his nose. "Well, no."

She handed the bottle back to him. "Then what the hell are you doing here, Cayden?"

Keane took the bottle back, looking more than a little disheartened. "Well, right now, I'm feeling a little kicked in the gut."

Lin sighed and stepped to the side, gesturing for Keane to step inside.

"Are you sure?" Keane asked. "This isn't going to end up

as some opportunity to take me down a few more pegs in private, is it?"

"That's entirely up to you," Lin said without any hint of humor.

"Right." Keane stepped inside and set the bottle of Relese Rosso down on the nearest table. "You know it's bad luck to give a gift back."

"That's not a gift."

The doors slid shut and Lin headed for the small kitchen, grabbing the bottle as she went.

"I paid hard-earned money for that," Keane said. "And I had no intention of keeping it myself. It's most certainly a gift."

Lin grabbed two glasses from the cabinet and poured them each half a glass. "Then it's a terrible gift."

"You've always been difficult to buy for," Keane said, taking his glass.

Relese Rosso is better at first sip. As it passes down through the drinker's palate it grows sweeter, before kicking back with one abruptly bitter bite right down the throat.

Lin didn't react as she drank it.

Keane winced horribly, having completely forgotten what it tasted like.

"Oh, this is awful," he gagged. "Why did I buy this?" He set the glass down on the counter and pushed it back towards Lin. "I'm not finishing that. In fact, I'm considering taking the bottle back and finding a black hole to drop it down."

Lin took another sip. "It's not bad."

Keane grimaced. "This is why I hate buying you anything."

"And yet, here you are, buying me something."

"Old habits die hard, I guess."

"Sure," she said, taking another sip. "Cavige confess yet?"

Keane shook his head. "And he probably won't. I don't think it matters, though. Zemble put together a pretty solid case. It should do most of the work."

"And what about the church?"

"What about it?"

"You came in here and stirred up a hornet's nest," she said. "I'm the one who's going to have to clean it up."

Keane frowned. "It's hardly a hornet's nest. Once Cavige gets transferred back to Earth for trial, the Church of Eternal Clarity isn't going to be bothered with sending anyone out here."

"Uh-huh." Lin sounded unconvinced. "What are you doing here, Cayden?"

"I come bearing good news," Keane said. "Turns out the case didn't have any classified implications attached to it. It's being kicked back over to the *Atlantic*. Not only that, but you get credit for bringing in Cavige." He held out his hands. "So, congratulations."

Lin finished her glass and pushed it off to the side. "I don't want credit for something I didn't do."

Keane shrugged. "Well, we can't really take credit for it. It would kind of defeat the whole purpose of being classified in the first place. Not that you heard any of that from me." He added that last part quickly.

"Right. *Classified*," she said. "Top secret. Hush-hush."

"I wouldn't be so jealous," Keane said. "It's mostly boring paperwork interrupted with momentary bouts of psychotic insanity."

She traced her finger around the rim of the empty glass, eyeing Keane from the kitchen. "Where does your makeover fall: Boring paperwork or psychotic insanity?"

"Makeover?" Keane asked in an unconvincing tone.

"Please." Lin came out of the kitchen and she poked at his chest. "How long have we known each other?"

"Too long," Keane said. "Way too long."

"You didn't think I wasn't going to notice there was something different about you?"

"Well, to be fair, most of it's on the inside," Keane said. "So, yeah."

"You walk differently. You carry yourself differently. Your hair has more color in it. You're missing some age lines." She leaned in and sniffed. "You even smell different."

Keane took a step back and cleared his throat. "This...is not why I came here."

"Of course it isn't. These days I hear you've got a thing for astrometrics ensigns who are nearly a decade younger than you."

Keane winced. "How the hell did you find out about that?"

Lin just frowned at him.

Keane shook his head, waving off the question. "Right. Never mind. Stupid question."

"So what happened?"

He looked down at his hands. "I honestly couldn't even begin to tell you and even if I did, I don't know that I should."

"Because it's *classified*?"

"Sure," Keane replied. "But psychotic insanity isn't exactly something that translates well secondhand."

"You've been docked here for two weeks and this is the first I've even heard from you," she said.

"I haven't been avoiding you."

"Yes, you have."

Keane sighed. "Well, yeah. Put yourself in my shoes and you'd probably avoid you, too."

She folded her arms again. "What the hell are you really doing here?"

Keane held up both hands. "I swear, I'm just here to make peace."

"Make peace," she echoed.

"I didn't want this to turn into some kind of territorial war between the *Atlantic* and the *Defiance*," he said. "We are all supposed to be on the same side, you know."

"Sure." Lin didn't sound convinced.

He leaned against the sofa. "You know, it doesn't have to be like this."

"I'm not the one avoiding you," she said.

"My ship is docked here."

"On my front door."

"You could have checked to see why I didn't come knocking."

"What is this?" she asked.

Keane shrugged. "Me just trying to avoid having you question me some more about my condition."

"If you don't want to talk about it, why are you here?" Lin asked.

Keane shrugged. "I don't know."

Lin nodded. "Heard you had quite the night before ending it with Ensign Mullins."

"It's starting to sound like you've been keeping tabs on me," Keane said.

"I started to get suspicious when you didn't stop by to say hi," she replied.

Keane opened his mouth and then shut it. He looked away, turning his gaze to the floor. "You know, I could probably get you in. I brought in Zemble. I could bring you in."

"I don't want in," she said. "I'm perfectly happy with what I've got here."

"I mean, boring paperwork and bouts of psychotic insanity." He looked up at her with a smile. "Maybe it's the winning combination you've been looking for?"

She stared at him for a minute, not saying anything.

"What?" he asked.

Lin shook her head and left the room.

"Are we done?" Keane asked.

Lin pulled off her top and tossed it to Keane. "We can be."

He stared at her naked back as she disappeared into the bedroom.

Keane looked down at the shirt in his hands and then up at the open doorway. "This isn't why I came here."

"Okay," she replied from the darkness of the room.

He glanced back at the closed front door, then at the shirt in his hands and then, finally at the open bedroom door.

"Okay," Keane said and tossed the shirt over his shoulder as he followed her into the bedroom.

32

STRAUB GOT up from her desk, ready to call it a night when her comm signaled an incoming transmission. Before she had the chance to deny it, a holographic image of an elderly man in his seventies appeared hovering over her desk.

"Kathryn, glad I caught you."

Straub hesitated, mostly from surprise, but also from frustration. The man in the hologram was dressed in a Fleet Admiralty uniform and the rank on his badge made it clear he was the Chief Fleet Admiral. He was balding, with a thick gray goatee and narrow eyes that seemed to only have one setting: disappointed.

He gestured to Straub's seat. "You might as well sit down, Kathryn. I'm not going anywhere until we have this conversation."

Straub mentally cursed to herself, but sat down anyway. "Admiral Perlman."

Admiral Stewart Perlman smirked at the tone of her voice and helped himself to a glass of water that was just out of the range of the holocam. "Well, I'm not too thrilled to have to have this conversation either."

Straub pressed her lips together. "What conversation would that be?"

Perlman frowned. "Don't play stupid with me, Kathryn. I'm live calling you from *Earth*. Do you know how much this call is costing the taxpayers? Let's do them a favor and cut the bullshit, okay?"

Straub shifted in her seat, feeling properly scolded. "Okay. So you've heard about Ambassador Reynoso."

Perlman snorted. "Yes. I've heard about Ambassador Reynoso. Would you like to know who I just got finished talking to before I called you up?"

"Clearly whoever it was, it wasn't a fun conversation."

"No, it was not," Perlman said. "I just got off the line with D'Ambra's Chief of Staff. Obie Daynard is not a pleasant man to talk to. Never mind his attitude, the man's lisp makes it nearly impossible to understand what the hell he's saying. Anytime I have to waste precious minutes talking to him, my day is generally ruined. It doesn't matter if I started off the day with some morning sex with my wife, a four-star diamond breakfast and news of the Rocket Devils finally winning the World Series. Five minutes with Daynard and my day is effectively shat on."

"My condolences," Straub said.

He glared at her.

Straub held up her hands. "I'm not sure what the hell you want me to say, Stewart."

"Right now, I really don't want you to say anything. I'm not charging the taxpayers this much to hear your excuses. This is a chewing out."

She sighed. "Look-"

Perlman held his hand. "*No*. You had an *ambassador die* on your watch. The Executive Branch doesn't like being the last to know when one of their valuable political appointees ends up *murdered*."

Straub snorted and rolled her eyes. "Valuable, right."

"Hey, I'm not joking around here, Kathryn."

"Neither am I," she said. "And they were hardly the last to know."

"That's not what they heard."

"What did they hear?"

"That you sat on Reynoso's death for over twenty-four hours before reporting it."

Straub didn't respond to that.

Perlman shook his head. "Damnit, Kathryn."

"It was a potentially volatile situation," Straub argued. "I made a call and I stand by it. Where did they hear this from anyway?"

"I don't know," Perlman said. "Clearly, on top of everything else you've got going on out there, you've got leaks to deal with."

Straub shook her head. "Somebody was going around leaking news of Reynoso's death to other dignitaries on the station."

"Kathryn-"

"I *know*. I am looking into it. Trust me, I know the problems with leaks out here."

"Daynard wants a head on a pike."

"For *what*?"

"For picking a fight with one of the largest religious organizations in the UPA."

"The hell I did."

"According to Daynard the Church of Eternal Clarity represents a rather considerable size of voters for D'Ambra," Perlman continued.

"Bullshit," Straub snapped.

"In addition," Perlman said, speaking over her curse. "The D'Ambra administration has, what Daynard describes, as a very healthy relationship with the leadership with the church. Or, at least they did until *you* had their leader arrested for murder."

"Last time I checked, that's how the system is supposed to work," Straub said. "You murder somebody, you get arrested. It's called justice. If it's a problem for anybody, it's going to be a problem for them."

Perlman leaned forward. "And they're going to make it a problem for *you*."

Straub didn't say anything for a moment. "If there's something you want to say, Stewart, you better come right out and say it."

"I'm pretty sure I already have." He sat back. "The D'Ambra administration doesn't like the Fleet. They've made that painfully clear over the last two years and it's not going to get any better. They're perfectly content making sacrificial lambs of whoever they damn well feel like, as long as it serves their agenda." Perlman's face set into a grim frown. "I wasn't born yesterday. I know Wanamaker's got some Directive Fifty-Two bullshit going on out there and I know you're in tight with him and Mitchell. But listen to me very carefully, Kathryn: You need to tread carefully and figure out where your loyalties lie."

"What the hell is that supposed to mean?"

"It means that there are some organizations that when you get into their crosshairs, there's nothing that's going to keep you safe." Perlman pointed at her. "Be careful, Kathryn."

Perlman blinked out as he severed the connection.

Straub sat back in her seat.

It suddenly felt like the middle of nowhere wasn't far enough away.

33

"Mr. Zemble."

Zemble looked up as Gavin Mitchell approached. "Captain," Zemble rumbled, starting to get to his feet.

Mitchell gestured for him to stay seated. "Don't bother getting up. You look comfortable and we're both off duty."

Zemble grunted, but settled back on the bench across from where the Atlantic Community Church used to be. "I think about that a lot."

"What?" Mitchell sat down next to him.

"Out here, we're never really off duty," Zemble said. "Especially you. You're always the captain. Sure, someone else can be in charge of the duty roster for a few hours, but you're still the captain. If a situation arises, you're the one who's going to handle it."

"Unless, of course, I get snapped away to some other dimension," Mitchell said, comfortably folding his arms.

Zemble grunted wordlessly.

Mitchell studied the empty facade across from them for a few seconds. "Mr. Zemble, I understand you've had a rough couple of days."

Zemble grunted. "What'd the old man tell you?"

"He told me you haven't seen the inside of your quarters in the better part of a week," Mitchell said. "You've been sleeping in Calloway's room in the medbay and as near as I can tell, you've been eating considerably less than you normally do." Mitchell paused and looked at Zemble's profile. "Although, to be fair, that's a hard one to gauge considering you don't look like you've lost any weight."

"Then how do you know I haven't been eating?" Zemble said, sounding more defensive than he intended.

"Because, despite what's said about me, I actually do pay attention to my people," Mitchell said. "So, seeing as I'm the only other person on the ship who's had experience with Steve sending them someplace they weren't supposed to go, I thought we should talk."

Zemble didn't say anything.

"I don't want to have to order you to talk to me, Zemble," Mitchell said. "It sends the wrong kind of message."

"Not much to talk about, Captain."

"Your behavior would suggest otherwise," Mitchell said.

"I'm not looking to pick a fight with anyone."

"Good. You shouldn't be. Neither am I. Is that something we need to talk about?"

Finally Zemble turned to look at him. "What are you doing here, Captain?"

"Exactly what it sounds like, Lieutenant."

Zemble grunted again and turned to face forward. "Do you believe in God, Captain?"

"Do I believe in God?" Mitchell took a second to sit on the question. His eyebrows went up as he stretched back on the bench. "That's a hell of a question."

Zemble nodded. "Usually always is."

"I'll be honest with you, Zemble, I don't really know how to answer that question."

"That's an answer in of itself," Zemble said.

"I suppose," Mitchell agreed. "Seems like a pretty weak answer, though."

"Men are weak creatures," Zemble replied.

"That's..." Mitchell shook his head. "I'm not sure how I'm supposed to respond to that."

"I believe in God," Zemble said. "I like to believe that I have a personal relationship with the Almighty Creator of the Universe. I like to believe that when I pray, He listens."

"And you don't think He does?"

"I don't know what to think anymore, Captain," Zemble said. "A little over two nights ago I stood here and met a man that I would arrest twenty-four hours later for the murder of Ambassador Reynoso. For some reason, that seems stranger to me than anything Steve did to me."

"I can see that."

Zemble looked at him. "Can you?"

Mitchell returned his gaze evenly. "Is there a particular answer you're looking for, Lieutenant?"

Zemble shrugged. "I don't know. Maybe that's the problem. Nothing feels right anymore. With all due respect, Captain, I don't think your experience when Steve sent you away is anything remotely like mine."

Mitchell smirked. "Is it supposed to be a contest?"

"No, but it would make things a lot easier to understand."

"For who? You or me?"

Again, Zemble shrugged. "I don't know."

They fell silent for another few seconds.

Mitchell ran a hand across his chin. "I like to think I believe in something more powerful than us."

"Steve was more powerful than us," Zemble said.

"That's technically true."

"The Devil's in the details, Captain."

Mitchell looked at him out of the corner of his eye. "Why does it feel like we're having two different conversations?"

"Because that's the point," Zemble said. "You want to help. You want to provide some kind of guidance. But, no offense, Captain, we're not even in the same book, much less the same page."

"Because of what?"

"Because it's not enough to believe that there's something more powerful than us out there," Zemble said. "It's a big galaxy. There's plenty of beings that are more powerful than us. You can't be agnostic out here."

"I disagree."

"That's why I haven't come to you for help."

"Wow, they weren't kidding when you said you were in a mood."

Zemble grunted. "People keep saying that."

"Well, if people keep saying it, maybe you need to consider the possibility that they're on to something, Lieutenant."

"I'll take it under consideration."

Mitchell shook his head. "I understand you've been running a Bible study on the ship."

"I was. We were going through the book of Philippians."

"What happened?"

"I got sent to some other dimension where time passed differently and I lost all sense of reality for what felt like decades," Zemble said. "When I came back, the Bible study didn't seem all that relevant anymore."

"Maybe that's part of your problem," Mitchell said.

Zemble looked at him, but didn't say anything.

"I'll be honest with you, Lieutenant, I don't know what I believe. The fact that you do believe in something and you believe so strongly, makes me kind of jealous. I think I'd like to have that kind of certainty about the way the universe works. But I don't and I'm not certain I can." Mitchell paused and took a breath. "I don't like the idea of turning my life over to someone like that. I don't like not having control. But most of all, it's been my experience that beings who go around proclaiming they're God usually end up just being little shitbags who are out to make my life difficult."

"That's not who God is," Zemble said.

Mitchell held up his hand. "I understand that. But, as I'm sure you understand right now, experience is a hard thing to overcome." Mitchell got to his feet. "Mr. Zemble, you are absolutely right: I'm not the person you need to come to in a time like this and I want to apologize for that. Because you're right about something else, I'm never not on duty. You're still my responsibility whether or not I'm on the clock and I'm sorry I can't help you. But I don't really think you need my help anyway. I think you're a stronger man than you give yourself credit for."

"What do you mean by that?"

"I mean that you think, on some level, God has abandoned you." Mitchell held up his hand again when he saw Zemble starting to talk. "But I don't think He has and, more than that, I don't think *you* think He has. But you think He *should*. Something happened to you in that dimension Steve sent you to, and since you've come back, nothing feels right, including your faith. And, because of that, you think God should turn His back on you."

Zemble turned away from Mitchell and stared down at his hands, not saying anything.

"I think you know that you're wrong," Mitchel said. "Faith is a funny thing, Mr. Zemble. After a certain point, I think it becomes instinctual. I think you should trust your instincts. They haven't let you down yet and I don't think God has either."

"You're not really agnostic, are you, Captain?" Zemble asked.

Mitchell held up his hands. "I don't know. My father was a pastor. I grew up in a very Christian household. At some point, I believe my father led me to be Born Again. I don't know if it stuck." He shrugged. "It is what it is, I suppose."

"If God hasn't given up on me, then He certainly hasn't given up on you, Captain."

Mitchell laughed softly. "I suppose so, Mr. Zemble." He clapped his hands together. "I think I'll leave you to it. Try not to be so hard on yourself, Zemble."

"Yes, sir."

Zemble watched as Mitchell walked away. As he disappeared around a corner, Zemble turned back to the church that was no longer there. He looked up at the faded outline of the cross and, for a split second, it seemed almost sharper, more defined than it had been a moment ago. Then Zemble blinked and it returned to its faded self.

Zemble nodded and got to his feet.

"Alright," he said. "Message received."

He started for the nearest lift and began to pray as he walked.

34

BENDARE WATCHED the news feed with a cold dispassion as a reporter announced the arrest of Joseph Michael Cavige and the deaths of Ambassador Reynoso and his aide. She was dressed in a white, fluffy robe that was nearly two sizes too large for her and her body disappeared beneath the robe, only the tips of her fingers were visible from beneath the sleeves. Her skin had lost that radiant glow, as though it was simply another form of makeup to be applied as needed. Here in her bedroom, wrapped up in her robe, and seated in an oversized chair at the foot of her bed Viv'an Bendare seemed less like a vivacious, sexpot crime lord and more like a young lady who just needed a sleepover with a few of her best friends.

Bendare fidgeted impatiently in her seat, watching the drama play out and finding the entire affair to be more anticlimactic than she would have cared for. As such, her attention kept drifting to the other screen.

On the second screen was a copy of the message Cavige had composed while posing as her, outlining the fake kameko drug deal Cavige had cooked up for Reynoso. Something about it appealed to her.

"Mr. Jacoby!"

From behind her, seated in the far corner across from the bed, the Vulderran rose up, setting aside the paper he was reading. "Yes, ma'am?"

Bendare didn't look away from the message. "Who do we have in the Veneer government right now?"

"No one," Jacoby replied. "All of our contacts went dark at the same time as the rest of the empire."

"What about that gentleman on the colony?"

"Aage Harrisson?" Jacoby said. "The freight captain for the Msmal Family?"

"Yes, him."

"He's dead."

Bendare twisted in her seat to look back at Jacoby. "Since when?"

"Since the colony was raided by the Syndicate and they killed everyone there," Jacoby replied.

Bendare sighed and turned back to the screens. "Right. The Syndicate." She fell silent for another moment, reading the message again. "You know, this isn't a half bad idea." She gestured at the message on the screen. "Why didn't we think about this?"

"Because, historically speaking, you're not fond of dealing with drugs."

Bendare plucked at her lower lip. "No, I suppose not."

"You tend to find the whole affair rather distasteful," he said.

"Well, it's important to have standards, Jacoby."

"I wholeheartedly agree."

"But this," she said. "There's something about this I like."

"I would imagine you find yourself attracted to the potential profits," Jacoby said.

Bendare nodded her head side to side. "Maybe. I suppose. Money is wonderful. But this isn't just about money." She gestured at the screen, waving her hand around in a circle. "This is about power. This is about *opportunity*. Untapped potential." She leaned forward. "I can't help myself, I like it. There's something clean about it."

"If you say so, ma'am."

"I do." Bendare folded her hands together under her chin. "So we've got no one in the Veneer government?"

"Nobody has anyone in the Veneer government," Jacoby replied. "Including the Veneer."

"Right. The Syndicate's running everything down there these days. Why haven't they gotten this? This is a gold mine, just sitting there."

"I can't recall with one hundred percent certainty, but I don't believe that anyone has ever accused the Oxean Syndicate of being smart," Jacoby replied.

"No, they have not," Bendare agreed. She sat back in her seat, crossing her legs. "We have somebody in the Syndicate, don't we? What's-his-face?" She snapped her fingers impatiently, the name just outside of her reach.

"Ma'cke'ns'on Fl'eu'ri'mond," Jacoby said helpfully.

"Yes. *Him*." She glanced back at Jacoby. "He's not dead, is he?"

"Not to my knowledge, ma'am."

"Good. Reach out to him. I want a meeting."

"And what shall I tell him the meeting is in regards to?" Jacoby asked.

Bendare read the message one more time. "New business opportunities."

35

"Mr. Warrick, when do you think my ship is going to be space worthy again?" Mitchell asked.

Warrick lay on his back, the top half of his body underneath a console near the rear of the bridge. Mitchell stood over him, arms folded as he leaned against the console under repair. Before Warrick could respond, there was a sharp electrical sound followed by a guttural curse from Warrick in a language Mitchell wasn't familiar with.

Mitchell felt the entire console vibrate and he took a step back. Half the console lit up and the other half exploded into a shower of sparks. Mitchell raised an arm against the sparks and took another step back.

"Mr. Warrick?" Mitchell asked. "Is everything-?" Before he could finish there was a loud *clunking* noise.

Warrick swore again and came out from under the console. His face was covered in black smudges and smoke drifted off his beard. He sat upright and held up a short cylinder with a black band wrapped around it and three red protrusions that looked like they were about to fall off.

He looked at Mitchell. "Do you know what this is?"

Mitchell studied the object for a moment and then shook his head. "I'm afraid I don't."

"Neither do I," Warrick said and tossed it into a pile of other pieces that had been pulled from various consoles on the bridge. The pile was suspiciously close to Mitchell's command chair and getting larger with every passing hour.

"That doesn't inspire a lot of confidence." Mitchell said.

"How do you think I feel?" Warrick asked. "I'm supposed to be your chief engineer and I genuinely don't know how this damn ship was pieced together. That's the third one of those things I've found. I think it might be an auxiliary microfilament processor. Problem is it's about eighty years old and nobody around here bothers to stay up to date on technology from eighty years ago. Whatever it is, it should have been replaced at least twenty years ago. I know what technology from twenty years ago looks like. Hell, most of the Fleet's ships were built twenty years ago and they're still in fine shape. In case you were wondering, this is not fine shape." He smacked the console and a small metal ball with half a dozen wires extending from it dropped from the inside, making a loud clattering sound as it struck the floor and rolled down to Mitchell's feet. Warrick pointed to the small metal ball. "Now *that*, I know what it is and it's not important."

"Is that supposed to reassure me?" Mitchell asked.

Warrick shrugged. "I can't recall, have I mentioned how we're way overdo for a refit?"

Mitchell frowned. "Yes, you've mentioned that. Multiple times."

Warrick nodded. "That's right, I have. And yet, nobody seems to listen to me."

"I listen to you, Mr. Warrick, I just don't have to follow your every suggestion."

"Suggestion? *Suggestion*? All due respect, Captain, this is less of a suggestion and more of a necessary requirement at this point," Warrick said. "There's only so many rolls of Qeebvavan tape that I can wrap around this bucket of bolts."

Mitchell held a closed hand to his mouth and cleared his throat. "Mr. Warrick, I don't think I should have to tell you this, but I can't run my ship in this condition."

"Well, at this rate, you're not going to be running your ship anywhere," Warrick replied, wiping the sweat from his forehead.

"Warrick..."

"You think I'm joking, but I'm not," he said. "I've got a crew working on the micro-fractures along the hull, so at least we won't break apart the next time we jump to light-speed. But the power system is still out of alignment. Every time I power up the ion drive we lose something."

"Such as?"

Warrick stroked his beard. "Well, this morning when we powered it up we lost life support on the starboard side of the ship."

Mitchell closed his eyes. "Warrick..."

"I am doing the best I can, Captain," he said. "But if you're expecting a miracle here, you're going to need to downgrade considerably. Like, a lot."

Mitchell pinched the bridge of his nose. "I'm not looking for a miracle. I'm just looking for a day when my ship can safely leave the *Atlantic's* dock without falling apart."

Warrick smiled wistfully. "Yes, that's the dream, isn't it?"

"Yes, as a matter of fact, it is, Warrick," Mitchell said. "And I want to know when that *dream* is going to become *reality*."

Warrick took a deep breath and did some mental calculations. "Five more days."

"You could have just said that at the start of all this," Mitchell pointed out.

"Obviously, I'd like more," Warrick said. "Say, a month or two."

"That's never going to happen."

"But I think I can get us back to something resembling normal-ish in five days," Warrick said. "Assuming, of course, I can get the power relays to stop blasting out like a couple of horny Nunzotov wildebeests and that I can keep Westin away from anything that she can blow up." He looked Mitchell directly in the eyes. "I need that woman off this ship before she kills us all."

Mitchell smiled. "One problem at a time, Mr. Warrick. One problem at a time."

"Then I vote we start with doing something about Westin," Warrick said. "Because if you can transfer her someplace else, I can probably get the entire ship turned around in forty-eight hours."

Mitchell clapped him on the shoulders. "Five days, Mr. Warrick. I'm going to hold you to that."

"I'm not joking here," Warrick said. "That woman is a genuine menace to us all."

"Captain? I have Commodore Straub on the line for you," the ensign on communications said.

Mitchell nodded to the main screen as he made his way around the pile of parts back to his chair. "Put her through, Ensign."

Straub appeared on the screen. She was on the command deck of the *Atlantic*. Behind her, Mallozzi was examining something that was just off screen. "Gavin, are you expecting any visitors?"

"Visitors?" Mitchell sat down and winced. He stood back up for a second and discovered a bolt in the seat of his chair.

He picked it up and tossed it back at Warrick. He turned back to Straub as he settled into his chair. "None that I'm aware of. What's going on?"

"A Natuzzi vessel just dropped out of hyperspace and is approaching the station," she said.

At the helm, Nax looked up in surprise. "I beg your pardon, Commodore, but did you say a *Natuzzi* vessel?"

She nodded and gestured to Mallozzi. "Marv?"

Mallozzi stepped up next to Straub. "They haven't hailed us yet, but according to their ship's registry they're flying under the Natuzzi Royal Parliament."

Nax immediately tensed up.

Mitchell leaned forward, folding his hands together. "This is a little outside the norm for most Natuzzi vessels. Any thoughts, Mr. Nax?"

"None that are coming to mind at this moment."

Mitchell turned back to the screen.

"Obviously it's not a coincidence that you have the one Natuzzi officer in the Fleet and this ship is parked outside on our front yard," Straub said.

"It's your house, Kathryn," Mitchell said.

Straub grunted. "Just make sure to keep me in the loop."

Mitchell nodded and the screen went blank as Straub cut the connection. He got up from the command chair and walked over to the helm.

"Mr. Nax, you're going to have to refresh my memory, but how often do Natuzzi vessels venture out this far from your home sector?"

"Not very often," Nax replied, his voice sounding slightly strained. "As I seem to recall, the last time a Natuzzi vessel came out this way was nearly thirty years ago and that was a science expedition to examine the Pàng Jù Nebula."

"So maybe they're just back out here to, what, double check their findings?"

Nax swallowed and kept his gaze focused on his console. "Unlikely as at the time the Natuzzi Science Institute found the entire endeavor to be a waste of time and resources."

"Yeah," Mitchell said. "It also sounds like something that wouldn't exactly fall under the purview of the Royal Parliament."

"No, it is not."

Mitchell frowned. "There has to be something you can share with me, Lieutenant."

Nax struggled to keep his expression neutral.

Mitchell leaned in and lowered his voice. "Nax, are we going to have a problem here?"

Nax looked at his captain, his expression blank. "I genuinely do not know how to answer that, sir."

Mitchell sighed. "Well, that doesn't inspire confidence, Mr. Nax."

"My sincerest apologies."

"Yeah, I'll keep those in mind," Mitchell said.

"Captain," the ensign on the comm spoke up again. "Incoming transmission from the Natuzzi vessel."

Mitchell drummed his hands on the side of the helm. "Alright, here we go. Put 'em on the screen, Ensign."

On the screen, a tall, orange skinned woman appeared. She was dressed in a white, skintight uniform with a single black band wrapping diagonally across her torso.

Mitchell greeted her with a smile. "Hi there. I'm Captain Gavin Mitchell of the *USS Defiance*. What can I do for you?"

"I am Glo Hol, First Commandant of the *Enlightened*." She spoke in a sharp, clipped tone that betrayed no emotion and no pleasantries. "We're here to take custody of the

Natuzzi male currently on your ship, his majesty Kinlin Nax."

Around the bridge there was a hushed murmur at the commandant's description of Nax.

Mitchell's smile faltered. He looked at Nax, who visibly winced and avoided the captain's gaze.

Mitchell drummed his fingers against the helm and turned his attention back to the screen. "Okay, well, there's a lot in there to unpack." He tried to stay genial about the situation. "I'm going to focus on the part where it sounds like you're trying to arrest a member of my crew. I think something may be lost in the translation here"

Commandant Hol bristled with a sour expression. "He may be a member of your crew, Captain Mitchell, but he is first a member of our race. I did not misspeak. You will remand him into our custody."

"Under what charges exactly?" Mitchell asked, all traces of pleasantries disappearing from his voice.

At this point Commandant Hol finally turned her gaze to Nax, as if acknowledging his presence. "Under Natuzzi Law his majesty Kinlin Nax has been charged, tried and found guilty of *High Treason*."

TO BE CONTINUED IN:
THE PRICE OF PARADISE

*Subscribe to my newsletter and I'll let you know as soon as the
next Defiance book is ready to read.*

Sign Up Here

https://onestrayword.beehiiv.com/subscribe

*Word-of-mouth is crucial for any author to succeed. If you
enjoyed this book, please consider leaving a review, even if it's
only a line or two. It would make all the difference and would be
very much appreciated.*

ABOUT THE AUTHOR

Jason Krumbine loves to write! He's happily married and lives in Orlando, FL where he enjoys visiting Disney World with his daughter and wife.

If you want to get an automatic email when Jason's next book is released sign up here:

https://onestrayword.beehiiv.com/subscribe

Your email address will never be shared and you can unsubscribe at any time.

ALSO BY JASON KRUMBINE

www.ingramcontent.com/pod-product-compliance
Lightning Source LLC
Chambersburg PA
CBHW031340020726
47499CB00005B/1352